THINK ME BACK

Think Me Back

CATHERINE FORDE

First published 2001
by House of Lochar

A CIP catalogue record for this book
is available from the British Library.

ISBN 1 899863 78 8

The publishers acknowledge subsidy from the
Scottish Arts Council towards the publication of this volume.

Typeset by XL Publishing Services, Tiverton
Printed in Great Britain
by SRP Ltd, Exeter
for House of Lochar
Isle of Colonsay, Argyll PA61 7YR

CHAPTER ONE

WHEN he first woke up, Pete Smeaton was sure he was still dreaming.

Then he opened his eyes and knew that it had really happened. He was lying in a sleeping bag on the floor of a room in his new home. A home he had never set eyes on before.

And Jenny was crying.

At least some things never changed.

Pete sat up stiffly and looked around. Whatever room he was in was furnished with nothing but packing cartons stacked one on top of the other. He couldn't tell if the room was large or small because all he could see were boxes, labelled in his mother's hasty scrawl:

Kitchen, My room, Hall, Pete, Jenny.

He remembered the hurried squeak of the marker pen on the boxes as the carrier waited to transport them up from London. That was just yesterday.

Even muffled by packing cartons, Jenny's cry was shrill and piercing. Pete groaned and flopped back on his sleeping bag. He closed his eyes and put his hands over his ears. The crying grew louder. Pete opened one eye, as Jenny was shoved into his arms.

'Take her, will you, so I can at least go to the toilet on my own. If I put her down she'll be sick. This new place is giving her the heebie-jeebies. She was up all night.'

Pete's mother left him with the hot, open-mouthed bundle that was his baby sister. Three months old and more hassle than twenty Petes had ever been, according to Mrs Smeaton.

Pete stared into the tiny, furious face.

'Hel–lo noisy,' he said slowly. Secretly, he loved the feeling of Jenny when he held her although he would never admit that out loud to anyone. No way!

Hearing Pete's voice, Jenny stopped crying instantly. Pete felt her body relax in his arms.

'Why d'you always stop crying for me, you little monkey?' Pete whispered on Jenny's downy head. 'You should give Mum a break.'

Fitting Jenny expertly in the crook of one arm, Pete levered himself up from the floor.

'C'mon let's see what this place is like, Jenny. Time to explore.'

The floorboards felt rough and chilly under Pete's feet. Snuggling Jenny close he went out into the hallway.

'Must have slept in the lounge,' Pete figured. He was downstairs and the only other room on this floor was a large square kitchen with a small scullery. Beyond lay a wild-looking garden.

'It's a jungle out there, Jenny,' said Pete in a American accent. 'Better wait till I'm armed before I investigate.'

Upstairs, on the half landing of the house there was a bathroom, and one huge empty bedroom. The morning sun streamed through its emptiness illuminating the motes of dust which danced in such numbers that the room appeared in soft focus.

Pete stood in the centre of this room and knew that he wanted it to be his. It was at least three times the size of his old bedroom in London.

Quickly, he planned where he would put his books and lean his guitar. His bed would fit perfectly in that corner over there, and if his desk fitted under the window he'd be able to look outside and daydream while he was supposed to be doing his homework.

There'd be enough room for all his friends to stay overnight if they brought their sleeping bags.

'We could have a midnight feast and make up all those

songs that drive Mum mad...'

Pete was whispering excitedly to Jenny. Then he remembered where he was now:

'What an idiot. What friends?' he said bitterly to Jenny. 'Don't know anyone here, do I? Never even heard of Clydebank before in my life. Don't even know what bloomin' school I'll be going to.'

Pete stared into Jenny's blue unblinking eyes.

'You're lucky. Bet we'll be back in London by the time you need any friends. How am I going to meet anyone here?'

Pete leaned his forehead despondently on the glass and stared down at the garden. It really did look like a jungle. An expanse of unruly grasses weaved before Pete, reaching down to a ramshackle brick outbuilding. Beyond that, the boundary of the garden was drawn by a row of mature trees and bushes.

'It's huge,' thought Pete, who had never lived in a house with a garden before. He had to admit – grudgingly – that this garden looked big enough for a decent game of football. It was his birthday next week. Maybe he'd ask for goalposts instead of that portable CD player he had his eye on.

Pete gazed out the window and saw himself running out onto the grass heading a crowd of boys:

'Good pass, Pete.'

'Here, over to me, Pete.'

'Yeah, nice one, Pete.'

'Pete, Pete.'

'Pete? Where on earth have you gone?'

Mrs Smeaton's irritation interrupted his reverie.

'What you doing with her now? It's all dusty up here.' She shuddered, 'Ugh! And chilly.'

Mrs Smeaton yanked Jenny from Pete's arms. She was asleep, a smug little smile playing over her lips.

'Now look what you've done,' Mrs Smeaton's voice rose in frustration. 'I wanted to feed her first.'

Pete shrugged, 'Sorry, Mum. She was awake two minutes

ago. Honest.' He was going to add, 'Got the magic touch, haven't I?' but something about his mum's pinched face and tired, shaky voice made him stop. She looked as though she was going to start crying again. He really hated that. Never could get used to it, even though she cried all the time these days. Her tears made Pete feel panicky and scared.

Quickly he asked, 'Mum, can I have this room if you and dad don't want it?'

'Do what you like,' snapped the answer. 'Won't make any difference to me. I don't sleep these days with this one yammering all the time. Someone in this family might as well use one of the bedrooms to get some rest.'

The bitterness in his mother's voice made Pete wince. He stood at the door of his new room watching her slump wearily downstairs with Jenny in her arms. There was a horrible tight feeling inside his chest.

By the time Mrs Smeaton had reached the bottom stair, Jenny was wailing.

'God sakes,' Pete heard his mother sigh, as she carried Jenny through to the kitchen, slamming the door behind her so hard that the whole house shook.

Then the wailing became louder. And louder still. It turned into sobbing. Huge, uncontrollable sobbing. Pete stood with his hand on the door knob and listened.

'Mum?'

Pete was more taken aback by the power of the crying than by the crying itself. Surely it wasn't Jenny? It was much too powerful. Whoever was crying was much closer than the kitchen downstairs. And it sounded like a child. Right next to Pete.

Through the tears Pete heard, 'Hooooo, no. I don't want to go. I want to stay here. Nooohhoo.'

Pete stood perfectly still holding his breath. It definitely wasn't Jenny, or his mother. Pete had the chilling sensation of a cold object running from the base of his spine, up over his neck, to the top of his head. At the same time an invisible hand rotated the contents of his stomach. He could not move because fear had drained all the power from his legs. He moved his eyes around the still, empty room. Between a break in the sobbing, Pete identified Jenny's sharp hungry cry far away somewhere downstairs. Then the other crying resumed, obliterating the sound of his baby sister.

It was a definitely a young cry, a child's, but not a baby's. It seemed to be coming, thought Pete, not from his room, as he first thought, but through the wall.

Slowly, Pete turned his head to the wall. Through the sobbing, a girl spoke.

'Oh please don't make me go. I want to stay here with you, Mummy. What if something happens to you?'

A second voice interrupted. This was a woman who spoke so gently, that Pete could not make out any words that were spoken. This voice soothed and shooshed the crying child for a long, long time, until Pete heard nothing but the gentlest of whispering, and the occasional breathless gulp from someone who was all cried out.

The hairs were standing up on Pete's arms. He had no idea how long he had remained with his hand on the doorknob.

But his fear had left him. The woman's voice reminded Pete of lying in his mother's bed when he was tiny, and listening to her voice as he drifted away from her into sleep. He remembered the delicious sense of knowing that everything was all right because his mother was there and would still be there when he woke up.

Whoever was through the wall could have fallen asleep too, because Pete heard a door being gently closed and light footsteps tapping away and downstairs into the distance.

CHAPTER TWO

PETE pressed his ear against the wall through which he had heard the crying. Listening hard, he thought he could just make out deep breathing and an occasional 'hic'.

'What the heck was all that about?' Pete muttered to himself. 'Thought Dad said we were the last house in the whole street. Must be people next door after all. Hope they don't go on like that all the time.'

Shaking his head in mystification, Pete wandered into the hall to look around the rest of the house. There were two more rooms on the top landing. One large and one much smaller.

His parents had slept in the largest room last night. A rumpled duvet was flung over two sleeping bags in the middle of the floor. Propped against a wall, was a mirror which had hung in the hall of the old flat. Several plastic bags spilling baby clothes and nappies were the only other things in the room, and it managed to look untidy despite its size.

Next door, Jenny's cot was tiny in the corner of another bare room. Pete picked up her teddy bear from the floor and looked out of the window. He was at the front of the house now, facing a wide expanse of grass even bigger than his back garden. This area divided Pete's street from a fast, multi-lane carriageway whose traffic noises Pete could hear from behind the glass in Jenny's bedroom. Beyond the road, soft, green hills met the sky and formed Pete's horizon.

'Bonnie Scotland,' said Pete, despondently. 'Looks nearly as busy as London.'

Staring dreamily at the distant traffic, the slam of a car door made Pete jump. Then he looked down at the pavement, and banged the window.

'Dad, up here!'

Mr Smeaton waved cheerfully. He carried a sheaf of folders under one arm, and several bags of shopping in the other. Pete ran downstairs to open the front door.

'You're awake, Pete-Smeet. Welcome to Scotland,' greeted Mr Smeaton, handing Pete his folders. 'What a big snoring sack of potatoes you were last night. Can't believe you didn't wake up when we arrived. I just chucked you down on the first floor I came to and left you. Didn't you hear Jenny screeching like a banshee in your ear as soon as we crossed the border?'

Pete followed his dad through to the kitchen helping him carry the packing crate containing crockery, cutlery, and a kettle from the piles stacked in the lounge.

''Fraid I've got to get on site this morning, Pete,' Mr Smeaton explained to Pete as he rummaged for cereal bowls and discovered a jar of instant coffee. 'I'll dive back when the furniture arrives this afternoon, but I might not be around much to give Mum a hand. So, Pete, will you… you know… do what you can. She's exhausted with Jenny just now.'

Mr Smeaton looked over to furthest corner of the kitchen. Mrs Smeaton had fallen asleep in a deckchair – the only seat in the house at the moment – with Jenny in her arms. Pete thought his mum even looked sad while she slept.

Mr Smeaton was staring too. He opened his mouth as though he was going to say something to Pete, but seemed to think better of it and instead, in an extra cheerful voice said,

'So Pete-Smeet, what do you think of your new house so far? Good when we get our own stuff in, eh?'

''S bigger than the flat,' said Pete without great enthusiasm, still watching his mother. Then he remembered his bedroom. 'But Mum said I can have the big room at the back. It's cool. Just hope that kid doesn't cry all the time.'

'Oh Jenny won't cry for ever. She'll soon realise she's up in Scotland now, and there's nothing to cry about any more.

Bit of colic, that's all that's wrong.' Pete noticed that his dad said the last sentence without conviction. Jenny wailed pretty much constantly whenever her father was around.

'No, not Jenny, Dad. The next door neighbour. Some girl. Not a baby. She was crying and crying about not wanting to go away somewhere. Then a woman came in and spoke to her till she stopped. Think she's gone off to sleep now. Her room must be right through the wall from mine. If she's going to cry like that I hope she does go away. Do my nut in, that crying.'

'Hang on, Pete.' Mr Smeaton frowned. 'There isn't anybody next door. We don't have any neighbours. What I mean is, this house is really kind of detached now. It stands on its own.'

'What d'you mean "now"?'

Pete wrinkled his nose and looked confused. He understood terms like 'detached' and 'semi-detached' and 'terraced' because Mr Smeaton was an architect, and Pete used to want to be one too, until he saw how hard it was for his father to find decent work.

'A house can't be kind of detached, can it? What are you talking about, Dad?'

Mr Smeaton said casually, 'Actually, Pete, there's a bit of a story about this house. I don't know all the details yet, but it's to do with history; what happened to Clydebank during the Second World War. I'll need to take you outside and show you what I mean, but let's have something to eat first. Jamie Milligan's coming by any time.'

Pete persisted. 'But Dad. I definitely heard people next door. I pressed my ear to the wall.'

Mr Smeaton put his hand on Pete's shoulder and said firmly, 'Mum must have had the radio on or something. I promise you, no one lives next door. Now, have I a treat for you, my boy?' Mr Smeaton opened a white paper bag and held it out to Pete.

'Take a sniff of these, Pete. You won't taste anything like

this in London. Scottish morning rolls. Now if only I could get this cooker to work, we could have had them with bacon and square sausage. If we had any bacon. Or sausage.'

Pete usually laughed at his dad's silly jokes, but not this time. He was thinking to himself:

'Dad's wrong. There's no radio in this house yet. Our stuff won't arrive until this afternoon.'

CHAPTER THREE

THERE was no chance to discuss the noises through the wall with Mr Smeaton again. As soon as his father had made something for himself and Pete to eat, he spread all the papers from his folders over the kitchen floor.

'I've to read through these plans before Milligan arrives. New boy has to make a good impression on his first day.'

Pete crouched down beside his father.

'Look at this place, Pete. Fifty major retailers. Multiplex cinema, sports centre. Some project.'

'Hmm.'

Pete, normally interested in his father's work, was still perplexed by what had passed earlier in the bedroom upstairs. He let his eyes go out of focus as he stared at the sleep-slumped figures of his mother and Jenny.

Then the doorbell rang, its unfamiliar jangle making Pete jerk out his leg in surprise. Coffee spread slowly over the plans on the floor.

'Pete.'

Mr Smeaton was on his feet, shouting into Pete's face. 'For heaven's sake. You clumsy diddy. That's Milligan. What's he going to say when he sees this mess? Oh, go and let him in while I get a cloth.'

Pete slunk miserably to the door. His father didn't get mad very often, but when he did it was horrible, especially when he was angry with Pete. Jenny was screaming in the background as Pete opened the front door, close to tears himself.

'Hello, there. Milligan. Jamie Milligan. Steve about?'

The tall man had swept past Pete with a proprietorial air leaving Pete bent double from a bone-crunching handshake administered as he strode by.

'Know m'way,' Milligan called back to Pete, as he swung open the kitchen door and boomed.

'Well, well, well. Happy families in here, isn't it? Rather you than me, folks.' he announced nodding towards Jenny and dramatically rolling his eyes at the ceiling, 'got my hands full enough with my ninety three year old mother. Who's this little rug rat making all the noise then?'

Pete surveyed the scene in the kitchen. Jenny, who had momentarily paused for breath, shocked by the sheer volume of Mr Milligan's commanding voice, now tried to see if she could shriek over him. She was never good with strangers. Mrs Smeaton, emerging crumpled from her much-needed snooze, was trying to lever herself from the deck-chair with as much dignity as she could. Her hair, Pete noticed, was all over her face, and she looked particularly dishevelled next to the well-groomed visitor in the smart suit, greatcoat and very expensive-looking tie. There was a big blob of baby-sick on her shoulder.

'Don't get up. Don't get up,' said Mr Milligan, at the same time helping to yank the bewildered-looking Mrs Smeaton from her low-slung seat.

'It's your good husband I'm here to see, so just ignore me,' he boomed so improbably, that the ridiculousness of the situation hit Pete, and he burst into a fit of hysterical giggles.

From the floor, Mr Smeaton knelt, barechested over the spoilt plans trying to mop up the coffee with his T-shirt.

'Jamie. Really sorry about this. No towel unpacked yet,

and Pete had a wee accident…' Mr Smeaton caught sight of Pete, whose hand was stuffed helplessly into his mouth as he tried not to laugh. He knew, from the mad, pop-eyed look in his father's eyes that the last thing he should do was what he was just about to do.

But Mr Milligan laughed, too. He knelt down on the floor and slapped Mr Smeaton playfully on his bare shoulder.

'Ouch!' thought Pete. 'Just as well he's the boss. Don't think I'd have done that in the mood dad's in.'

'So this is what you think of my new shopping centre,' said Mr Milligan, producing a monogrammed handkerchief and helping Mr Smeaton blot the paper. 'Trashing my plans, are you?'

Mr Smeaton tried to explain, 'It was an accid…'

Mr Milligan turned to Pete and winked conspiratorially, 'Lucky I've brought a set of new ones. Some of the measurements have been changed by the Council since we last spoke. Here. These are the latest blueprints, and I need to go over them with you down on site soon as poss.'

Pete saw his father's face crumple with relief. He dropped his head sheepishly.

'What an impression to give you, Jamie. Thought I'd go over these while I grabbed a bite with Pete. But he's too busy telling me about kids crying through the wall, and not listening when I tell him there's no one there.'

Mr Smeaton had dragged Pete playfully towards Mr Milligan in a neck hold. 'You did introduce yourself to Mr Milligan, Pete, didn't you? You know, he's my new *Boss*. The one I have to make a good *impression* on.'

Pete knew by his father's mocking tone, that he was forgiven. Mr Smeaton was smiling now as he pulled a woozy-looking Mrs Smeaton towards Mr Milligan and introduced her.

'This is Jo, my wife, but because of this one,' he shouted playfully in Jenny's crying face, 'she'd rather be Rip Van Winkle these days.'

'Hello, Mr Milligan,' said Mrs Smeaton, shaking his hand dopily. 'Sorry, you've not caught us at our best. Thanks for sorting us out with the house. It's... it's lovely,' she added unconvincingly. 'Well, once we get our furniture in, it'll be great.'

'Lovely to meet you. Welcome to Scotland,' Mr Milligan said to Mrs Smeaton. Pete detected a change in his manner. He wasn't talking so loudly any more, nor was he really listening to what Mrs Smeaton was saying although he smiled at her genuinely enough. He seemed distracted as he told her to let him know if there was anything needing sorted with the house, anything at all. All the time, he kept glancing uncertainly towards Pete.

Mrs Smeaton was forced to take the screaming Jenny upstairs to be changed and fed. Mr Smeaton spread the new plans over a cupboard in the scullery and settled down to study them out of harms way. Pete found himself alone with Mr Milligan.

'What's all this about crying through the wall, Pete? What did you hear?'

Mr Milligan was frowning slightly. He asked lightheartedly enough, but there was an earnestness in the way he spoke. Pete wasn't sure if he was angry with him, or worried. Maybe the people next door are Mr Milligan's tenants too, Pete thought. Maybe he'll chuck them out for being noisy neighbours.

From the kitchen his father answered for him.

'I told Dolly Dimple that no one lives next door. Must have heard a radio, or Jenny, or alien voices in his head or something. Don't listen to him.'

But Mr Milligan had placed his hand on Pete's shoulder.

'Did you here a girl crying, and a woman's voice? Did you, Pete?'

The eyes that met Pete's were troubled, the face pale beneath the golfer's tan. Mr Milligan was on the point of saying something else to Pete, when a pager bleeped at his waistband.

'Damn.' He grabbed it and read the message.

'Don't tell me! Big problem, Steve. Gotta run. I'll get back to you pronto. See myself out.'

Pete followed Mr Milligan to the door, several paces behind his flapping greatcoat. He seemed unaware that Pete was behind him, but just as he was about to close the front door at his back he spoke, without turning round,

'Wait till my mother hears that Beth's back.'

CHAPTER FOUR

'LOOK out, Pete, there's a tiger,' joked Mr Smeaton, scything a path through the back garden with his legs. 'Wonder if we'll find any friends for you hiding in here.'

'Huh, fat chance!'

Pete followed his father through the undergrowth, forcing the sharp green stalks aside. The long-undisturbed grasses sliced at his hands in protest at the intrusion.

'Milligan's going to send someone round later to tidy this up for us,' said Mr Smeaton. 'He's seems a pretty decent guy so far.'

'Hmm,' said Pete, thinking of Mr Milligan's words as he left earlier. He didn't know what to make of his father's new boss.

'Good size isn't it, Pete? We've never had a proper garden before.'

They moved slowly to the back of the garden where trees and rhododendron bushes formed a natural border. Mr Smeaton turned Pete round to look back towards the house. And what Pete saw then made him gasp. Before he could say anything, his father was explaining.

'Remember I said there was a story about this house, and

you were going on about neighbours. Now you can see that there couldn't possibly be any.'

Pete nodded with his mouth open. He faced the right hand side of what had once been two houses joined together to form one large semi-detached house. But the left side no longer existed. Pete could see it had once been there by the ragged brickwork which brought his side of the house to an abrupt end. Huge metal and wooden props shored up the Smeaton's half of the building.

Some way down the street there was a similar house which was intact and which Pete guessed was how his house should have looked had half of it not been – well, he had no idea *what* had happened to it.

'Come this way, Pete,' said Mr Smeaton, leading his son across the neglected garden and through to where the other half of the house would have stood.

They stepped over a mound of jagged bricks and into a gravelly space between two of the biggest wooden props. Here, the ground sloped downwards into a deep crater.

'Our house is half of what used to be two semi-detached villas, but in 1941 it was bombed by the Germans. The whole of Clydebank was bombed in fact. You've heard about the Blitz in London, haven't you? Well, Clydebank was practically destroyed. Only eight out of twelve thousand homes were undamaged in two nights of bombing. Unbelievable, eh? This whole community was ripped apart.'

Pete looked around him in silence, listening as his father's words echoed around the ruin where they stood.

'Our new house is unusual. It's quite far from where most of the damage was done in Clydebank. And unlike most of the houses that were bombed, it's never been rebuilt. You can see it's part of a row of Victorian houses, and it was the only one in this street to be completely destroyed.'

Pete stood in the ruins of the bombed house and looked up at what had once been the internal walls of a house that joined on to his own new house. He could count the rooms:

there was the front lounge. He could see the outline of where the fireplace had once stood, the chimney now exposed. The kitchen would have been there. And he could trace the ascending pattern of the stair treads, the stonework charred black. Pete identified the bathroom by the pieces of green tile on a section of wall, and scraps of floral wallpaper probably hung in that bedroom which would have been through the wall from his own room.

Pete shivered. The room markings on the jagged exposed walls stood out vividly despite the attempts of sprouting weeds to hide the evidence of an existence torn down by the giant hand of war.

'What happened to the people who lived here? Were they in the house when it was bombed, Dad?'

Pete's question ricocheted around the vacant space.

'No idea, Pete. I'd like to find that out too. Milligan'll be able to tell us. It's his mother's house, you see – our side. She lived in it till recently, but she's in a home now. Apparently she refused to let them pull her side down after the war because it wasn't damaged and she wouldn't leave it. Milligan had it modernised last year so he can let it out. He said he could never sell it.'

'He probably doesn't want to stay in it himself because it's going to topple over, or it's haunted,' said Pete, with a shudder.

'Nah,' said Mr Smeaton, 'told me it was too big for him. He lives in some penthouse he designed in Glasgow.'

'Does Mum know about the state of this place? What does she think about living in a house propped up with sticks next door to a place where a load of people might have died? We might be standing on a graveyard for all we know. Ugh, it's horrible, Dad.'

Pete scrambled quickly from the ruins to his own garden. His father came after him and steered him through the undergrowth again.

'C'mon Pete, before you jump to conclusions, I want to

show you something else. Another bit of history. And by the way, of course your mother knows that the house is propped up, you daftie. We'll ask Milligan all about the bombed house when he comes back. He's going to give me gen on schools for you, you know.'

Pete groaned. It seemed like ages since he had been to school although it had only been a few days. He had had to say goodbye to all his friends in a hurry. That had been hard. Probably wouldn't see any of them ever again. Simon and Alfie had been his best friends for three years.

Mr Smeaton had turned up at school two days ago to take Pete home to pack and leave for Scotland that very evening. Everything happened as quickly as that.

When Pete was called out of class he thought something was up with mum or Jenny. Then dad told him in the head's office that he was leaving RIGHT THEN and if he wanted to say goodbye to any of his friends, this was his only chance. That *was* nearly as bad as something happening to Mum or Jenny.

Everyone was looking at him and he stood out in the front of the class and said, 'I'm going away to live in Scotland. My dad's got a job.'

He looked at Simon and Alfie and he wanted to go over and say lots of things to them, in private, but he didn't. He couldn't. Just said, 'Well bye, everyone.' and gave a sort of half wave with his hand and left the class with his head down.

All the way home in the car Pete had kept his eyes closed tight, talking into himself to Simon and Alfie. His dad said maybe Simon and Alfie could come to stay once things got settled. But Pete knew that would never happen; they were too far away now.

He didn't want to pass the swimming pool where he'd swum thousands of lengths for his club, or the tennis courts where he played with mum before Jenny was born, or the cafe where he drank Shirley Temples with Simon and Alfie.

He just kept his eyes shut, wishing that when he opened

them he would be sitting in class beside Mira with the gold bangles which tinkled like music, listening to Mr Fielding telling him to 'Pay attention, Smeaton. AHEM!'

But here he was, two days later, standing in his new garden in Clydebank worrying about starting yet another school – in a different country for goodness sake where everyone spoke with a Scottish accent. Nobody would understand him. And they would tease him about his London voice, even more than his dad did.

As Pete followed his father back through the garden he said, 'I'll have to start talking like you do, Dad. You'll have to teach me how to talk Scotch.'

'Scot-tish, you mean. Don't worry, you'll soon lose that London accent and I can call you my son at last. If this job goes well, we'll be able to buy our own house up here. Maybe out in the country. But look Pete, this is what I wanted to show you.'

They were at the ramshackle outhouse Pete had seen from his window. Up close, it was bigger than it looked. The rusty, corrugated metal door, complained as they swung it open and went inside. The roof, also corrugated, seemed intact, although Pete could see chinks of daylight through gaps in the sheets. The building was about twice the size of a large garden hut. It was bare inside, except for two rows of slatted wooden seats which ran the length of the walls on either side.

'D'you know what this is, Pete?' Mr Smeaton asked.

'A cool den for me,' answered Pete, eyes wide both to accommodate the gloom, and with excitement.

'Could be,' answered his father, 'but this was once an air raid shelter for the houses round about. During the Second World War, whenever the sirens went off, people would have to run down here and stay, sometimes for hours, until the all-clear sounded. There can't be many of these buildings left. I'm amazed this one's survived.'

'Maybe Mr Milligan's mother wanted to keep it,' said Pete. 'Can I use it as a den, Dad?'

Pete was already making plans about what he could do in a place like this.

'Well, I'll check with Milligan to make sure that it's safe, and that he has no objections. Wouldn't be surprised if he spent quite some time down here when he didn't want to. No harm in asking him. But, Pete, the reason I showed you this shelter is to tell you that whoever lived through the wall from us when the bomb dropped on the house was probably safe in this shelter at the time.'

Pete looked solemnly at his father.

'I'm going to ask Mr Milligan that, Dad.' Then he brightened, 'Can I borrow your torch? I want to check out this place properly.'

Cheerfully Pete walked back towards the house with his father to collect the torch. He wondered if his mother would give him some old carpets to floor the shelter, and if there was any chance of getting power in there. He hoped nobody else had a claim on it.

He brushed the stalks in the garden with his hands, lost in thought, and almost missed the figure that made his father stop in his tracks and charge across the garden towards the ruined house.

'Where'd she come from? Oi!' shouted Mr Smeaton, running with difficulty through the tangled undergrowth.

Against a backdrop of large trees, Pete glimpsed a woman dressed in long floaty garments of pale colours. She was too far away for Pete to determine if she was young or old, and by the time he had blinked, she was gone.

He watched his father stumble towards the spot where she had stood, and then when he lost sight of her, plunge his way back towards Pete.

'Where'd she come from?' he said. 'And where'd she go? There's nothing beyond those trees but open fields. We're at the end of a cul-de-sac.'

CHAPTER FIVE

PETE emptied his sports bag of the clothes he had brought with him last night, leaving in his Walkperson, as his mother insisted on calling it, his football sticker book, and his favourite wrestling figures. He grabbed a roll, a banana, and a can from the kitchen. Then, as an afterthought, he picked up an old rag which lay by the sink. The shelter had looked a bit cobwebby and if there was one thing Pete couldn't stand, it was cobwebs.

He strode purposefully through the garden towards his new den feeling surprisingly happy. It was sunny. His new house was fine – at least, it would be when all the furniture arrived – and his room was excellent. Even better, dad had a job again, so he would be happy, and although Pete knew he would have to face going to a new school, he didn't need to worry about that until after the Easter holidays which were just about to begin. All he needed now, really, were a few friends.

Pete sighed at that thought, and his optimism shrunk inside him like a deflating balloon.

If only his new den was back in London.

What Simon and Alfie would say if they could see it!

Simon would get his mum to make them all outfits so they could pretend they were soldiers rescuing victims of an air raid. Alfie would want to tell scary stories about people who had died during the war, spooking everyone so much that they would all have to go out into the garden in a posse if one of them had to pee. It would be great.

Pete wondered what Alfie would have to say about the sobbing that came through the wall from a room that didn't exist any more. Then he made himself stop wondering: he had to sleep in that room tonight, after all.

Pete was in the doorway of the shelter by now, adjusting his eyes to the dimness. In his mind, Simon and Alfie were at his shoulder, looking in behind him. That is why he was not more surprised when a boy came hurtling towards him from the back of the shelter.

'What you doin' here? Gerrout. You're trespassin' pal.' The boy advanced in a very un-pal-like manner coming to a halt about half a millimetre from Pete's nose.

Pete was taken aback by the presence of this stranger. The boy had a deep, growly voice, with an accent like Mr Smeaton's, but rougher. He was no taller than Pete, and a good deal thinner.

'I live 'ere, don't I?'

Pete tried his toughest South London accent, which was nothing like his real voice. He let his words dangle menacingly on his lower lip and he hung his arms long at his sides the way the hard nuts in his old school used to do. Inside he prayed that he didn't sound posh.

The boy stared into Pete's face trying to make out his features in the gloom.

'No. *I* live here, as a matter of fact,' said the shadowy stranger, in an altogether less confident and not nearly so rough voice.

'See. That's m'back garden there.'

He moved outside and pulled back a rhododendron bush at the back of Pete's garden revealing a large lawn bordered with well-tended flower beds and adorned – Pete noted for future reference – with a giant-sized trampoline.

'This is *my* garden you're in just now, and this den belongs to it.'

Pete indicated the overgrown chaos behind him, wishing Milligan's lawnmower man had arrived.

'We just moved up here last night.'

The stranger couldn't help but look interested.

'Where you from, then? You talk dead funny?'

'London.'

'You don't talk like people from London, like in East Enders, 'n' stuff like that.'

Pete was secretly delighted.

'M'dad's Scotch. His mum lives in Milngavie. He sounds like you.'

The boy seemed satisfied with this answer.

'Och, you're only half-English, then, and you sound a bit Scottish – don't say Scotch up here by the way.'

'Sorry,' said Pete, adding pointedly, 'But this *is* my den. M'dad said it was an old air raid shelter belonging to the two halves of our house.'

'Yeah, but it was used by the houses on *our* side too,' said the boy, an edge in his voice, 'and I've lived here since I was two; that's nine years, you know. It's always been my den.'

He looked challengingly at Pete, but his face was kind and Pete thought he looked like good fun. He had coppery red hair, a complexion that seemed to be crocheted in freckles, and dark brown eyes. Something about him reminded Pete of Simon.

'We're the same age,' said Pete. 'I'm eleven too – well I will be next week.'

The boy looked at Pete, and said nothing.

'Suppose we both use the shelter. What about that?' Pete suggested.

The boy still said nothing. Critically he looked Pete up and down.

'D'you like football?'

'Yeah, it's brill. Support Scotland, you know,' Pete replied, enthusiastically.

The boy nodded approvingly, still considering the deal on offer.

'D'you like music?'

'Yeah,' Pete's eyes lit up and he took a step nearer. 'I want to be a Rock star, like Elvis or the Beatles. I can play some of their stuff on the guitar. My dad's teaching me.'

'*Who* do you like?' The boy was unimpressed. 'I was meaning like *real* pop stars; Robbie Williams and Ladzlife. Don't you like all that stuff? I want to be a drummer.'

'Cool,' said Pete, 'But all that stuff you like's not as good as the older stuff. All the new bands just recycle the sounds of the past. Well, that's what my mum and dad say, anyway. Hey. Maybe we could get a band going in here, and we could play really loud and no one would complain. I'm getting a portable CD for my birthday. Well, I might be.'

'Lucky you. Wish I'd a drumkit,' added the boy. 'I keep asking for one but my mum and dad ignore me.'

'They always do that and think you don't notice,' Pete sympathised.

The two boys faced each other, eyes shining. Then at the same moment they both laughed.

'Ach! Let's share the den,' said Pete's new friend. He held out his hand to Pete. 'I'm Jimmy Dunn, but everyone calls me Dunny.'

'DUNNY?' Pete exploded with laughter. 'D'you know what your name means?'

'Yeah! Nothin',' said Dunny, looking annoyed at Pete's hilarity. ''Sjust my nickname.'

'A dunny's a toilet,' laughed Pete. 'That's the word my dad uses. Well, in Scotch – I mean Scot-tish – it means a cellar, but in Australian it means toilet.'

'Well, I don't know anything about that,' said Dunny dismissively. 'Everyone in our family is called Dunny. M'dad, m'cousins. M'wee brother's not called Dunny though. He's Wee Stookie.'

'Wee what?' asked Pete, glad to move on from the touchy subject of Dunny's name.

'Stookie. He's always breaking bones and having to get another stookie from the hospital.'

Dunny tried an exaggerated English accent.

'A stookie's a plaaaaster, you know. Yeah, my li-il bruvver; he's awnly fawr and ee's broken bowf 'is legs, ee 'as, an' 'is arms, 'is nose an' 'is ankle. Wicked innit?'

'Cool!' said Pete. 'I slid down some stairs in a cardboard box once, and bit right through my lip to the other side, but I haven't ever broken anything.'

'Me neither,' Dunny admitted in his normal voice.

'Anyway what's your name? Bet it's Algernon, or Cecil, or something dead posh like that. Or I know, bet it's Ni-gel.'

'I'm Pete,' laughed Pete. 'Peter Smeaton. Dad calls me Pete-Smeet, but everyone else calls me Pete, except Jenny, that is. She's my sister, but she's only three months old and can't talk yet.'

'Just wait till she starts,' groaned Dunny shaking his head wisely, as if he had expert knowledge. 'She'll never shut up.'

'Have you got sisters?'

'No way, man. Just know she'll never shut up. The girls in my school are like that.'

'Why aren't you there today, Dunny?' asked Pete.

'In service. Then two more days, and then the Easter Holidays. Yesss!'

'I'm on holidays, too,' said Pete. 'Then I've to start a new school,' he groaned, 'But I don't know where yet.'

'Oh, just come to my school,' said Dunny generously. 'I'll tell everyone not to laugh at your voice now that I know you're OK. And I won't let them call you Ni-gel.'

'Thanks,' said Pete, gratefully.

'What you brought with you?' asked Dunny, pointing at Pete's bag.

'Oh, nothing much,' said Pete, feeling rather embarrassed about the things he had presumed to bring to someone else's den. Dunny, however was impressed.

'Whoaw. WWF wrestlers. All right! Love these. Collect these. I've got hundreds, and all the videos and the Playstation games. Look.'

He delved into the furthest corner of the shelter and dragged out a plastic ice-cream tub from which protruded an entanglement of burly plastic arms and legs.

'Let's have a Royal Rumble,' said Dunny. 'Here's the ring.'

He produced a dusty miniature wrestling ring. 'All my friends are fed up with wrestlers now, but I still think they're brill. Oh, ace!' he held up Pete's Walkperson.

'Is this yours?'

'And I brought a torch,' said Pete, nodding.

Dunny flicked it on, and immediately a little circle of space near the door where the boys crouched was bathed in weak yellow light.

Dunny continued his investigation of the contents of Pete's bag.

'Only one measly roll and a can of Coke. You'll need to do better than that from now on if you want to share this den with me, pal.'

The boys laughed.

Pete swung the torch around the den to get a better look. Although the surfaces of the slatted wooden benches around the walls were empty, underneath they were stacked with boxes and boxes of toys.

'Is this all your stuff?' asked Pete.

Dunny nodded, concentrating as he set his wrestlers in position.

'My mum hates toys lying around. "If I trip over them, they go in the bin." That's what she says. She likes everything tidy. M'dad says it's because she's a New Rotic and he says he likes to keep out of her road and Wee Stookie and I should do the same if we're smart. I keep everything down here, so she doesn't chuck it out. And it's away from Wee Stookie. Think he comes down here, though, because my stuff's always moved about from where I left it. Right. AND HERE THEY COME. OH NO! IT'S STARTED. THE CROWD ARE ON THEIR FEET.'

Dunny was crouched on his knees waiting for Pete to challenge his wrestler. Pete noticed with a shiver that there were cobwebs spun between the elastic bars of the wrestling ring.

He found the rag he had brought.

'Don't think I'm soft, will you, but I hate cobwebs.'

Pete brushed away a large web, careful not to let his fingers touch any of it. 'These things give me the creeps,' he explained.

'Oh, Ni-gel, they can't harm you,' said Dunny, but not unkindly, swiping the palm of his hand unceremoniously along the bars on his side of the ring, then wiping it clean on his sweatshirt.

'Tell you somethin', if you hate cobwebs you won't want to see the notebook I found in here last year. It was *covered* in cobwebs, and there were loads of dead insects squished between the pages, and it stank. Even I didn't want to touch it. I just picked it up by the teeniest corner I could get, had a quick swatch at what it was about, and stuck it into a plastic bag. Reckon it's an important document, y'see. YES! AND HOGAN TOMBSTONES AUSTEN FOR THE SECOND TIME IN THIS EPIC BATTLE OF THE CHAMPIONS. LET'S TAKE A LOOK AT THAT AGAIN IN SLO-MO.'

Dunny pulled back the arm of his wrestler and punched Pete's man in the face sending him clattering to the back of the den.

'AND ONCE AGAIN, HE CATCHES AUSTEN OFF GUARD.'

'What d'you mean 'Important Document'?' asked Pete.

'Well, it was written in here for a start. Mum told me. Then she told me to chuck it away and wash my hands with disinfectant because it was filthy and full of germs. Should have seen her face when I brought it into the house; you'd have thought it was a dead cat full of maggots, or something. I didn't throw it out though; thought I'd better keep it.'

'What was the point of that?' snapped Pete. He was annoyed at how quickly Dunny had beaten his wrestler.

'*I* could write something in here and leave it lying about on this grotty floor for a few days till it went all gunky. That hardly makes it an important document.'

'Ah, but you see,' explained Dunny importantly, rummaging in one of his boxes and pulling out something wrapped in a see-through plastic bag, 'this wasn't *my* notebook. It belonged to somebody who wrote it during the Second World War.'

A little shiver of interest and something else – maybe fear – ran through Pete. He took the bag from Dunny, recalling his earlier conversation with his father.

'Actually,' Dunny continued, warming to his subject, but at the same time busy setting up another wrestler, 'I even think I know who wrote the notebook. And I reckon she got killed.'

He had lowered his voice, making Pete look up sharply.

'Who?'

'I think it belonged to *your* next door neighbour.' Dunny looked triumphantly at Pete nodding his head up and down in a 'what d'you have to say about that?' kind of way.

'I don't have a next door neighbour. The house was bombed,' said Pete, aware of an uncomfortable prickling sensation in his scalp. His mouth was dry.

'Not now, you don't, but during the war there must have been a girl who lived in the other half of your house.'

'You mean the side that was…'

'Yeah, blown up. *BOOM*!!!!' interrupted Dunny.

The two boys looked at each other. Pete daren't give voice to his thoughts.

'D'you think she was, y'know, killed by a bomb?'

He was whispering.

'Dunno,' said Dunny. 'Probably.'

'How d'you know she lived next door to my house?' asked Pete. 'Could have lived in *your* house and used this shelter, couldn't she?'

'Ah, but she's put her address at the beginning of the book. Look.' Dunny opened the front cover. '14 Cairns Road. I live in Alder Place.'

'And I'm at 12. She was my neighbour.' Pete gave a low whistle.

The atmosphere in the shelter had changed. The wrestling match lay abandoned on the floor, and both boys had risen to their feet and were staring at each other, breathing hard. They whispered, although there was no need to do so.

A little tape in Pete's head replayed the noises he had heard through his wall. He tried to ignore it. He slipped the notebook out of the bag on to the floor. The edges of the pages between the hard cardboard covers were curled at the top and bottom making the paper squash inwards like a concertina when Pete picked it up.

He flicked through the book. Most of it was blank, and all the pages were stained with watery brown damp spots. He moved from the back cover to the final entry, and started to read:

'"*It's horrible down here*" – I can hardly read this writing, it's so curly – "*Everything's crashing down outside. Really, really near. The ground's shaking...*"'

'Yeah, yeah, it's all about the air raid and how she'll miss mummy because she's being sent away, boo hoo hoo. Pretty boring really, and not much else further back in the book either, but see this too.'

Dunny had pulled Pete by the wrist and led him to face the back wall of the shelter. He moved Pete's torch around to light the wall.

'The girl who left the notebook, did this. Look!'

Pete hunkered down and peered at the wall.

'You're right. Same writing,' he said.

Several neat lines, written in thick black pencil were clearly legible on the wall. Next to the writing, were drawn a line of funny little characters: gnomes, animals, elves, little chubby fairies with curly hair and wizards with magic wands. There were about a dozen drawings in all, obviously the work of a child, but comical and clever.

'She did this,' said Dunny, tapping a name written at the end of the lines of drawing. 'It's the same girl who wrote the notebook; she's put drawings just like these in it. And it's the same handwriting.'

'They're pretty good aren't they?' said Pete. 'What does this say?'

He read the pencilled words aloud:

> '*Adolf Hitler don't strike here*
> *Take your bombs and disappear*
> *You are hateful, you are bad,*
> *When we beat you, you'll be mad.*'

At the bottom, the author had drawn a simple cartoon face which Pete recognised as Hitler. A big black cross ran through the face, as if a hand had scored hard and angrily on the wall.

'"Beth Winters", that's the name of the girl who wrote that. "Beth Winters",' said Dunny pointing the name out. 'Look, she's written it here on the wall, and her age, "eleven years and one month old".'

'She's even put the date,' said Pete, squinting down at where the writing became small, and moving the torch over the words, '"13th March 1941".'

'Sixty years ago exactly. To the day,' emphasised Dunny, tapping a finger on the side of his nose mysteriously. 'And it's the same date as that last entry in the notebook. Look.' He swung the torch on to the notebook again and flicked to the entry he had been reading. '"13th March 1941".'

Pete shivered. He said quietly, 'All a bit spooky isn't it? Wish I knew what happened to her?'

'Well, the 13th and 14th of March was when Clydebank was destroyed in the Blitz,' said Dunny.

Pete nodded. 'I only knew about the London Blitz before, but m'dad told me about what happened here. 'Bout how only eight out of twelve thousand houses weren't damaged.'

'Yeah, and nearly a thousand people killed,' said Dunny. 'Pretty bad for a small place like this.'

'Beth Winters,' said Pete quietly. 'What about her, I wonder? Was she one of the thousand?'

The two boys looked at each other. The shelter had become dark and chilly.

'Well, she wasn't in the house when she wrote *this*,' said Pete, unconvincingly, putting the notebook back in the plastic bag. 'So maybe she survived.'

'Who knows,' said Dunny. He shivered, 'Brrr, freezin' down here. Listen, let's go out and play in my garden for a while. Fancy a bounce on my trampoline?'

Pete was glad to leave the shelter then. While he'd read Beth's poem and looked at the notebook, he was thinking about the crying through the wall. Should he tell Dunny about it, he wondered? Part of him was frightened to bring the matter up. Better not, he decided. Didn't want his only friend to think he was a fruitcake and disappear as soon as they had met.

Grabbing the banana from his bag, Pete followed Dunny who had already squeezed himself through a gap in the hedge into his own garden.

'Hang on, Dunny,' said Pete, 'I'll have to tell mum where I am, or she'll go nuts.'

Pete thrashed through his own garden stuffing banana into his mouth as he ran. 'Mum. Dad,' he spluttered, trying his back door. Locked.

'Darn it.'

Pete hurried around to the front of his house taking the route over the ruined side of the building. His feet slid over the uneven ground sending small stones bouncing into the bomb crater.

Watching his footing and peeling back the banana at the same time, Pete almost headbutted the woman who stepped out from the ruin in front of him.

Elderly, but not old looking. Soft, floaty clothes in summery blues and purples. Faded blond hair coiled peculiarly in plaits around each ear Princess Leia-style. Pete computed these details about the stranger while a disturbing voice whispered in his head:

'She's the woman Dad saw earlier.'

'D'you know, when I was your age, I didn't see one of them for four years.'

She was pointing at the banana. And she spoke with a really weird accent. When she said 'years', her voice went up at the end as though she was asking a question, not making a statement.

Pete took a step backwards and looked around him, as though he expected someone familiar to materialise and help him out.

'Whenever I have one now, I slice it up into as many pieces as I can and eat them one by one.'

The woman giggled to herself, and then fixed Pete with serious blue eyes.

'You haven't come across a... an old box, an old shoebox around here, have you?' Pete swallowed hard and shook his head. He moved past the woman round to his front door.

'I haven't,' he said ringing the bell urgently. 'Just moved in. But hang on and I'll ask my mum.'

He rang the bell again, and again, aware of the strange woman standing a little distance away from him, watching.

'Mum,' he yelled, thumping the glass on the door with his fist, 'Open up! MUUUU...'

'...UUM.'

Mrs Smeaton flung the door open furiously as Pete yelled full in her face. Jenny was yelling incredibly loudly from upstairs.

His mother's voice crackled above Jenny's screaming, 'What the heck d'you need to bang and ring like that for, Pete? Listen to that. I'd just gotten her off to sleep. You just never ever THINK, do you?'

Pete was indignant.

'Couldn't get in the back, and that woman was asking me things, and I wanted to get YOU to speak to her, like I'm supposed to, but I won't BOTHER next time!'

Pete flung out his arm dramatically indicating the spot

behind him where the woman had hovered.

Mrs Smeaton stepped outside, Jenny's bawling reverberated around the cul-de-sac. It was deserted.

'Was there someone here, Pete?' asked Mrs Smeaton, concern in her voice, 'I don't see anybody.

Pete wasn't there to answer. He had stomped angrily up to his room and slammed the door as hard as he could.

As it closed, he remembered what Mr Milligan had said as he shut the front door behind him earlier on.

Something about telling his mother that Beth was back.

CHAPTER SIX

PETE muttered to himself as he fiddled with the catch on his window.

'Why's she always mad these days? She'd have been even madder if she'd caught me talking to that weird woman.'

'I'm sorry, pet.' Mrs Smeaton came into the room. Jenny was still crying. Pete heard tears in his mother's voice. He didn't want her to cry.

'I just wanted to know if I could go in to play with my new friend, Dunny, and then that woman stopped me. I didn't want to talk to her on my own.'

'Pete, you were doing the right thing, and I shouldn't have yelled at you. There's no one there now, though,' said Mrs Smeaton. 'Now who's this new friend? Toilet did you say his name was?'

Pete laughed. 'Dunny didn't know that's what his name meant till I told him,' said Pete, 'and he wasn't too happy. His real name's Jimmy Dunn. We're the same age, and he likes wrestlers. And he just lives over there.' Pete pointed towards Dunny's garden from the window.

'That's nice, dear,' said Mrs Smeaton wearily.

'I just came back to ask permission to go into his garden.'

'I'd like to meet him before you go to his house,' said Mrs Smeaton, 'and check that it's OK with his mum. But Dad and I could really do with you here right now.'

As if on cue the doorbell rang.

'That should be our furniture men arriving. Thought that was them ringing and ringing the bell when you came in, and I was about to give them a right mouthful. You got it instead. You'll need to see Dunny later. Come on downstairs with me and let's get to work.

'Excuse me.'

At the foot of the stairs, Dunny's red head poked around Mr Smeaton, who was standing with the removal men at the front door discussing where everything should go. He spoke in such a posh voice that Pete snorted with laughter.

'Can Pete come out? My mum says it's all right for him to come round to my house.' Dunny came right inside when he spotted Pete on the stairs.

'Hello, Ni-gel,' said Pete sarcastically, making Dunny blush, 'who's a terribly posh little fellow all of a sudden?'

'Sorry, son, Pete can't come out,' said Mr Smeaton, shaking Dunny's hand, 'but you can come in if you like, providing you've got energy, muscles, and a mum that won't mind.'

For the next three hours, everyone worked like Trojans, unpacking familiar objects and finding new homes for them. After a bit of expert rocking from Pete, Jenny fell asleep and stayed asleep throughout the bustle and scraping and thumping. This was despite being tickled and poked by Dunny who kept tiptoeing up to her cot to see if she was awake yet. When he saw her in Pete's arms for the first time he lifted her tiny hand and whispered, 'Oh, she's gorgeous.'

'Thought you didn't like girls,' Pete reminded him.

The boys helped Mr Smeaton arrange the furniture in the lounge and then, once Pete's wardrobe and dressing table were carried upstairs, they unpacked the crates with PETE written on then.

'I'm glad you chose a pal with muscles,' Mr Smeaton said, squeezing Dunny's bicep every time he puffed past him with another load.

'This is brill fun,' said Dunny, taking a rest at last and looking out of Pete's bedroom window towards his own back garden. 'I'm going into the removal business when I leave school. Nothin' to it and all the lifting'll really help my wrestling.'

Pete joined Dunny at the window. They watched a small boy with tousled red hair jumping on the trampoline.

'Wee Stookie,' said Dunny. 'Let's see if he can hear me from up here.'

Dunny flung Pete's window open.

'How d'you manage that?' asked an astonished Pete. It had been stiff as anything.

'Muscles, mate. Good Scottish muscles. Hey, wee guy. Stookie, lookie! Up here! Look!'

The tousled head could be seen turning round to see who was calling him. He kept on jumping at the same time. A dark haired woman who was hanging up washing in the garden also turned. They both spotted Dunny, and raised their arms to wave. Next moment there was a blood-curdling scream. The tousled head didn't bounce up again. Pete and Dunny watched as Mrs Dunn dropped the T-shirt she was holding and rushed towards the trampoline.

'Crikey,' said Dunny turning from the window. His face had turned so pale that his freckles had disappeared. 'Wee Stookie's had another one. And it looks like my fault.'

Downstairs he ran, thrashing through Pete's garden towards the awful shrieking of his brother.

Bushes partly obscured Pete's view of Dunny's garden. He swithered about whether or not to go down and see if he could do anything to help.

Very close by a girl's voice spoke.

'Mummy, can you help me? I don't know if I've put in the right clothes.'

Pete's blood ran cold. He could hear the words spoken much more clearly than the last time. They were only slightly muffled, as though uttered through a cardboard tube. With his eyes still fixed in the direction of Dunny's garden, Pete moved over to the wall which divided his house from what was once next door. He put his ear to the plaster. Quite clearly he heard someone moving about. Bedsprings creaked, and wood grazed wood as a drawer slid open. He heard an exasperated sigh, and then a loud and impatient, 'MUM-MEE!'

Then silence.

More silence.

And through the silence floated the notes of *The Skye Boat Song* played slowly and haltingly on a recorder. The music was so clear that Pete could hear the musician draw breath between bars. He was sure that a swipe of his hand through the wall would have brought him face to face with the musician. But of course he did not do this. Instead he held his breath, aware of adult footsteps clicking up the stairs. He heard the squeak of a door so near him that he swung round to look at the door of his own bedroom expecting his mother to walk in (although she wore shoes that clomped rather than clicked).

The playing ceased mid-note. Pete heard a woman's voice; the same voice he had heard earlier, its timbre light and pleasant.

'Here's something else to take with you, Beth, so you won't feel too homesick.'

Pete did not catch the reply, because through his open window he heard Dunny yell up at him.

'Pete, can you come down here, a minute? Wee Stookie's hurt pretty bad.'

CHAPTER SEVEN

BY THE TIME Pete got downstairs, Dunny, close to tears, was explaining to Mr Smeaton, 'Wee Stookie's fallen and the bone's poking through his arm. My mum's in a panic.'

'Let's see what we can do,' said Mr Smeaton. He followed Pete and Dunny through the garden.

They pushed through the bushes to where the dark haired woman who had been hanging out the washing, now crouched over a sobbing child.

'Hi. Steve Smeaton,' said Pete's dad, briskly, kneeling beside Wee Stookie. 'I've met your other son, and who's this then?'

'Mark,' sniffed the woman. 'I'm Carol and it's broken, isn't it?'

Mr Smeaton was trying to examine Wee Stookie's arm without moving it.

'He'll have to go to casualty right now. I'll take you; we'd be longer if we wait for an ambulance. Dunny can stay here with Pete, if you don't mind. My wife's at home.'

Carol sniffed and nodded.

'My husband's away, and I don't drive. That would be great.'

'C'mon then. Up we come soldier.'

Mr Smeaton lifted Wee Stookie very gently. He groaned in pain.

'Meet me at the front of my house,' said Mr Smeaton to Carol. 'This fellow'll be fine, and we'll take good care of Dunny. He's already done our removal for us, so its the least we can do.'

Pete and Dunny followed Mr Smeaton to the car. Wee Stookie was silent now, shivering and very, very pale.

Pete looked at his small, frightened face and felt sorry for him.

'D'you like wrestlers?' he asked him, and without waiting for an answer, he ran down to the shelter to pick up his favourite men from the floor.

Someone was already inside. Pete stopped dead in the doorway. Through the dim afternoon light which filtered through the gaps in the roof, Pete saw a girl at the far end of the shelter. Her back was to him. She was kneeling on the floor and writing on the whitewashed wall.

Pete's entrance disturbed her. She turned sharply and stared at him, rising to her feet at the same time. Quickly and silently she brushed past him and disappeared into the garden, flicking one of her long, blond plaits over her shoulder at the point where she was closest to Pete, like a cat switching her tail in indignation. The bristly, weighted tip of the plait stung Pete's cheek reproachfully. Raising his hand to his face to rub the spot, he had no time to register surprise, or fear, or to challenge the girl as to what she was doing in his shelter. It was all over so fast.

Dazed, he stooped to pick up the wrestlers for Wee Stookie, and as he did so, a black pencil fell from the bench and rolled to a stop at his feet.

Pete picked it up and ran quickly to the car. Disturbed by the strange girl, he managed a weak smile as he passed the wrestlers through the window to Wee Stookie.

'Good luck,' he called as they drove away.

Dunny shook his head despondently, watching the car until it disappeared.

'Mum's gonna be in some state,' he said. 'She's never away from that hospital with Wee Stookie. And Dad's never around when she needs him. Well, he's just never around.'

The boys made their way back into Pete's house.

'Who's going to look after your sister while your mum's at the hospital with Wee Stookie?' asked Pete.

'What?' asked Dunny, absently, turning to his friend. 'Told

you already I don't have a sister. Don't you think a wee bampot brother like that's bad enough?'

'So who's the girl who was in our shelter? She was writing on the wall when I went in to get the wrestlers for Stookie. She dropped this. Look.'

Pete held out his hand and showed the black pencil to Dunny.

He took it and turned it over in his hands, examining it.

He stared at the pencil and, without looking up, spoke,

'No girls round here, Pete. No way. Only old folk and a few babies. Sometimes my pals go down the shelter, but only if I let them. But look, Pete. The name on this pencil. D'you see it?'

Dunny held the pencil close to Pete's nose and ran his fingernail under the faded gold lettering embossed on the pencil.

It read 'Elizabeth Winters'.

CHAPTER EIGHT

PETE didn't know what to make of the pencil, or this Beth Winters who had dropped it. Although his common sense told him that there was nothing through his bedroom wall, his gut reaction – which he tried to ignore, but couldn't – told him something else.

He pondered all this as his mother marched him and Dunny along the canal path which led from the end of Pete's road into the main shopping centre in Clydebank. Even if he'd wanted to discuss the crying girl with Dunny on the way to the shops – and he was still concerned that Dunny would think he was flaky and have nothing more to do with him – he would have been too out of breath to do so.

Because she was furious – again – his mum. Just before Wee Stookie had his accident, she had been about to go out shopping, on her own, in the car. Instead she had to drag the baby, the buggy and the boys with her. Not a good combination given her present state of mind.

Taking directions from Dunny, she had hared along the canal walkway into the centre of Clydebank, racing the buggy at such high speed that Jenny's eyes watered, although she was too startled to cry.

When Mrs Smeaton had bought as much as she could possibly carry on one trip, and a little bit more, in case she didn't get out again for a few days, or all the shops went on strike, she divided all the bags up between the handles of Jenny's buggy and the boys and yomped back along the canal path even faster than before, leaving the laden boys struggling behind.

'She's given us millions of bags. Does she think we're bloomin' Gladiators or something?' groaned Dunny.

Pete sighed in agreement. With his mother a speck in the distance by now, he felt uneasy as he laboured along the dingy walkway past the upturned trolleys and bicycle wheels which littered the filthy canal.

Huddles of older-looking boys in tracksuits and baseball caps turned and scowled with open hostility at Pete and Dunny as they went by.

Someone kicked a stone as the boys passed. It struck Pete's ankle. Flushing angrily, he looked round.

'Oot helping yer mammy, ye saddo nancies?' a voice growled.

'Keep going,' panted Dunny, 'Don't look. They're neds from my school. And they're all mental.'

Tucking their heads down, Pete and Dunny moved as fast as they could without actually breaking into a run. Neither boy turned around until they reached the end of the canal pathway and came off it and into Pete's road.

The cul-de-sac, with Pete's house at the end was invitingly

quiet and empty. There weren't even any cars parked on the road; the only vehicle was Jenny's empty buggy, wheels upturned under the weight of bulging shopping bags. Pete's front door was open. He could hear Jenny screaming inside before he had even crossed the street.

The boys staggered into the hallway with their shopping bags.

'Get the rest for me, Pete. This one's ravenous,' said Mrs Smeaton.

Dunny stayed in the kitchen and started unpacking.

'D'you think if we started screaming we'd get some food right away?' grumbled Pete to Dunny. He was tired and starving. 'I'll make us some cheese toasties. No point in asking Mum to do it.'

Pete went outside and crouched down to pick up the buggy and bring it inside.

When he stood up, he found himself looking into the pale blue eyes of the woman with the funny voice and the Princess Leia hair. Everything about this woman seemed out of place, not least her flowing, colourful clothes, so light and so different, Pete realised, from the dull tracksuits he had seen on the canal path and drab, anoraked shoppers in the supermarket. This woman, thought Pete would not have looked at all out of place in his old neighbourhood in London, full of ethnic shops and colourful market stalls.

'Excuse me,' she said in that strange, sing-song voice. 'I'm looking for Jamie. Does he still live here? He might have found my box you see.'

The woman looked searchingly into Pete's eyes.

'Jamie? Jamie Milligan, you're not his son. No, no you couldn't be. You see, I'm looking for something... oh, I don't know.'

Pete stared blankly at the woman, wondering what to say. He thought she looked a bit sad, and worried, the expression in her eyes old and young at the same time. The way she stared at Pete reminded him of Jenny.

'I… I… I'm Pete-Smeet,' he stammered, using his father's pet name for himself. 'I told you. I've just moved in. Wait here. I'll get m'mum.'

Pete went into his hallway, his head half-turned towards the woman to see what she would do next. Without taking a step, she inclined her body forwards, calling after Pete's retreating back,

'It's all right, Pete-Smeet. I'll come back and see you later.'

'No. Wait. Mu-um!' Pete yelled, 'There's a woman at the door. What's your na…'

He turned back to check that the woman was still there.

The cul-de sac was empty.

'Who is it?' called Mrs Smeaton from the kitchen.

'Dunno, she's gone,' Pete yelled back. He swung himself out of the front door, holding on to the side post, and looked up and down the street. Deserted.

'Where's she gone?' he said to himself, wandering back into the kitchen. Dunny was still unpacking the shopping while Mrs Smeaton sat in the deckchair feeding Jenny and directing him.

'Woman in funny clothes, all bright and colourful like she came from somewhere foreign,' said Pete.

Dunny paused at the open door of the fridge, milk carton in hand.

'Did she sound different, like when she talked?'

Dunny put the milk he was holding in the fridge and turned to look at Pete.

'Did she have a funny accent? I mean English, but like she was on Neighbours or something.'

'We don't watch that nonsense,' said Mrs Smeaton quickly, 'but I know it's Australian. Did this woman sound Australian, Pete?'

'Don't know any Australians, do I?' said Pete. He felt annoyed with himself for letting this woman get away again.

'I've got an uncle in Auckland, and that woman talked a bit like him,' said Dunny.

Mrs Smeaton laughed, 'Except Auckland's in New Zealand, not Australia, and I don't think the Kiwis would be pleased if you thought they were Aussies. It's a bit like being Scottish and being called English. You know how your dad feels about that.'

'Anyhow,' said Dunny, 'I think I've seen that woman before. It must be the same one; floaty clothes, funny accent. Weird hairdo, like ...'

'Princess Leia,' said Pete and Dunny in unison.

Dunny looked from Pete to Mrs Smeaton.

'That's her. She was in your garden last week, down by the old shelter. I didn't know she was there until she called over the wall while Wee Stookie and I were bouncing on the trampoline. She gave us a fright, calling through the bushes and Wee Stookie took a dive off and busted his nose. While I was kneeling down beside him she kept calling through the bushes, asking me if I'd found some box she'd lost. "Deed you fayend eet? Deed you fayend eet?"' Dunny attempted a Kiwi accent. 'There was blood everywhere, as usual, so I just yelled at her "no missus" and ran to tell mum about Wee Stookie. When I came back she was gone. Disappeared. Ali Kazam.'

'Sounds like the same person,' said Pete, opening a packet of chocolate biscuits. 'And she asked me about Jamie. But I don't know a Jamie.'

'Not round here,' said Dunny, shaking his head. 'And we know that's not you coz you're Nigel.'

'Well, I'm not happy about anyone hanging around here speaking to children,' said Mrs Smeaton. 'If you see her again, don't talk to her, d'you hear me? Neither of you. Get me or Dad, or your mum right away, Dunny. OK?' Mrs Smeaton levered herself out of the deckchair. 'I do believe this child is full.' She snatched the packet of biscuits from Pete. 'Let me make you boys something decent to eat.'

While they were eating, Mr Smeaton arrived back from the hospital.

'That's a brave brother you've got, Dunny', said Mr Smeaton washing his hands. 'No way Pete-Smeet here would've kept from bubbling like your Wee Stookie did. Need to call him Big Stookie now; wait till you see the plaster he's to wear. Right up to his neck.'

'Shouldn't have shouted at him out the window like that,' said Dunny. 'I'm away to see him. Thanks for the toastie, Mrs Smeaton.'

'Nice boy that,' said Mrs Smeaton when Dunny had gone. 'Very well trained about the house. Hope some of it rubs off on you guys. Was very glad to have him today when I went SHOPPING.'

'Ouch!' said Mr Smeaton ducking behind Pete. 'That poisoned arrow was for my benefit, I think, Pete.' He spread his hands out in a gesture of helplessness. 'What could I have done? The child was hurt and the mother needed help. You should see the state that *she* was in, poor woman. They gave her a real hard time at the hospital, and wanted to know who I was too.'

'I'll bet they did. Mr Great-at-looking-after-other-people-and-other-people's-children.'

Pete sensed the mood in his kitchen change, turning sour.

'You're so hail-fellow well-met with other people. "Milligan" *this* and "Jamie" *that*. What about when your wife needs you?'

Pete let himself out the back door, as his mother's voice rose to a peevish whine. Why, since Jenny was born, did she act as though everyone was trying to make her life harder? *She* would have taken Wee Stookie to hospital herself if she got to him first. And Dad wasn't always going on about 'Milligan' *this* and 'Jamie' *that*. Wait a minute. Pete stopped and said aloud.

'Jamie. That woman was looking for Jamie. That's Milligan's name. It's him she wants.'

Pete turned back towards his house to tell his mother. His hand was on the back door when he heard his parents' voices shouting inside. His mother's shrill angriness punctuated by his father's deeper tones. Both voices getting louder.

With a sigh Pete wandered slowly down to the shelter. The torch lay on the floor. Pete slumped on one of the benches and aimlessly flicked it on, letting the thin yellow beam play over the whitewashed walls. It found the rhyme he and Dunny had read that morning, and the date: '13th March 1941'.

Pete lingered there, fixing his eyes on the date until they went out of focus. After a while, he closed his eyes, feeling the lids heavy. He was tired, very tired. He let the back of his head rest against the rough wall behind him and he raised his face upwards letting his mouth relax. Through a gap in the roof of the shelter a shaft of sunlight bathed his head. The torch drooped loosely in Pete's grasp as he let his mind open to the twists and turns of a stolen daydream.

He was travelling at first, which is how his daydreams often began, this time fast along the motorway from London to Scotland; faster than he wanted to. His eyes were closed but in this special dreamlike state, Pete could see everything he passed as though he had x-ray eyes.

Strange things, that his sensible self knew would not be on the motorway, were dotted along the hard shoulder, like the stall he had set up on the M1 selling off all his wrestling figures. He saw himself sobbing at the roadside as he passed, and heard himself shout through tears that his mum said he wasn't to bring any toys to Clydebank because she was a New Rotic and wanted everything to be tidy from now on.

Wee Stookie was bouncing up and down behind Mrs Smeaton while she was talking, eating a banana. He wore his hair in long blond plaits and they kept flicking out and catching Pete in the eye even if he turned away.

Pete tried to open his mouth to ask his dad to stop the car so that he could get out and buy the wrestlers back from himself, but when he tried to speak, not only were his lips glued shut, but he could not make himself heard above a screaming, wailing siren which seemed to flood every nerve in his body, bombarding him with an inescapable sense of panic. And with this panic came fear. Yet Pete could not move. His heavy limbs and even heavier eyelids seemed to work like magnets, holding him prisoner on the bench, unable to wake, unable to move.

Pete struggled with his dreaming self, terror mounting as the noise of the siren continued to blast through his ears. He wondered why his parents didn't come running down to see what was the matter, and then he told himself, of course they can't, silly, because this is only happening to me in my head.

Pete was aware of a change in the air around him. The heat which had bathed his head so pleasantly now seemed to have suffused his whole body and intensified to an uncomfortable level. The fresh spring air in the shelter smelled stale as though it was being shared by many people. In his daydream Pete sensed someone moving towards him from further along the bench. Whoever it was came very, very close to him. Pete's nostrils picked up the unmistakable nip of urine, familiar to him from Jenny's nappy. An open-mouthed child rasped so close to Pete that hot sweet breath condensed on his face.

Pete, although his eyes were still closed, knew there were others around him besides this child. And everyone including himself was afraid.

The siren stopped wailing, the silence which followed as it cut out almost as unbearable as the noise it replaced. Pete tensed as a vibration rippled his seat and grew to a rumble. Then he heard planes passing overhead lower than he thought any plane should or could fly. More silence then, hanging like curtain of dread around the shelter. Pete knew that he was waiting for something bad to happen and he tried to brace himself, but his body was soft and asleep.

Beside him, the rasping breath became a whimper.

Loud muffled thumps were heard very near the shelter. A woman said urgently, 'Jamie pet, come here and stay by me.

Beth, darlin', are you all right? You stay by me, an' all. You're shakin'.'

Then there was a great bang. Pete jumped, opening his eyes wide. The torch fell with a clatter to the floor, the light going out. Pete was alone in the dark, empty shelter.

Breathing hard, he flicked the torch around the shelter walls.

There were new lines written there. In the same handwriting as before. This time, though, it looked as if the pencil trembled over each word:

When you are here and I am far away
Think me back and I will make my thoughts fly
To be with you and hold your hands.

This was signed, in an even shakier hand:

For Mummy and Daddy, with love from Beth.

CHAPTER NINE

PETE exhaled slowly, and with his finger traced the words on the wall. The hairs on the back of his neck were bristling.

'Hiya!'

The small figure at his elbow had crept up on Pete so silently that Pete nearly had heart failure when it spoke. His first thought was 'Jamie', but then he saw the large plaster and recognised the freckled face of Wee Stookie.

'Sign m'plaster?' he said, thrusting his arm under Pete's nose. 'Do somethin' dead rude.'

'Hi, there,' said Pete, gently lifting up Wee Stookie's arm which was indeed plastered from hand to shoulder.

'My bone was sticking right out,' said Wee Stookie,

impressively. 'You could see all the muscles and stringy bits inside.'

'Mmm, yummy,' said Pete as Wee Stookie giggled, 'Mum spewed up into one of those wee cardboard hats that was supposed to be for me, and she was pure affronted. They'd to take her away and clean her up.'

Wee Stookie sniggered.

'Even yummier!' said Pete.

'Here, sign it. Your dad's already done it, and Dunny – he drew a big bum under his name. Look, here's the doctor's signature – Dr Dempster – he was funny.'

'Right,' said Pete, looking for a good patch on the plaster to write something. 'Let's find a good spo… Crikey! Who did this?'

His blood ran cold. Across Wee Stookie's knuckles someone had drawn a very clever cartoon of a boy caught in mid-air as he fell off a trampoline. Although the drawing was tiny, it had caught the unmistakable likeness of Wee Stookie's muscular legs and curly hair. Even his freckles.

'Your sister, of course. Why does she keep doing this with her hair?'

Wee Stookie handed Pete his red biro and then gave an exaggerated performance of someone flicking hair haughtily over each shoulder, turning his head to the right and left just as Pete had witnessed Beth doing in front of him.

'Nearly poked my eye out, so she did. Didn't you hear her outside? I asked her to sign my plaster and she said she couldn't because that posh boy made her drop her best pencil. Then when she saw my biro she said she'd use that instead of a pencil because she'd never used anything like that before. Bit bonkers, is she?'

Pete gulped, and examined the drawing on Wee Stookies arm. 'I'm not posh,' he mumbled.

The style was unmistakably that of Beth Winters. She had even signed her name with a tiny flourish, just like on the shelter wall: *Beth Winters*.

'Where'd she go?'

'Back home, of course. She peeked into the shelter first but didn't go in. Have you fallen out with her or something?'

Wee Stookie was squeezing backwards through the bushes into his own garden. Only his head protruded as he talked to Pete. He was like the Cheshire cat.

'My mum says you can come over to play any time you like, s'long as you take your shoes off at the door,' said Wee Stookie withdrawing his head still further until only his mouth and chin remained visible. 'Don't bring flicky pigtails though. We don't like them, me 'n' Dunny. Girlies. She wears dead stupid clothes, by the way. Ah mean, that kilt's pure sad, man. Tell her that if you like. I don't care.'

'She's got nothing to do with me,' said Pete in a small voice.

'Who was wearing stupid clothes? You still on about that Australian woman, Pete?'

As Wee Stookie disappeared through the hedge the elder version of him pushed his way into Pete's garden.

'Pure sad that kilt,' Wee Stookie's voice could be heard to say.

'She's not my sister,' Pete shouted after him, and then more quietly to Dunny, looking straight at him, 'She's not my sister.'

'What's up with your face, Pete?' asked Dunny.

'She was here again, Dunny. Beth what's-her-name. Signed Wee Stookie's plaster, and look,' Pete dragged Dunny to the back of the shelter and showed him the new verse which Beth had written. 'That wasn't here before, was it?'

Dunny examined Beth's latest verse, and then he read it out in a silly high voice, '"*To be with you and hold your hands. For Mummy and Daddy.*" PUKE. What a stupid soppy ejit. Blargghh.'

Dunny staggered dramatically out of the shelter. Clutching the wall he pretended to vomit spectacularly.

'Blargghh. Puke, Huey. Why are girls so soppy?'

Pete followed Dunny meekly outside, surprised by his

reaction to the poem which he had thought actually quite sad – although there was no way he was going to admit that to Dunny.

'D'you not think it's a bit, well, spooky, that this girl keeps appearing now? I mean, it's her stuff that we're reading on the wall, and we know she lived in the half of my house that got bombed, and we don't know whether she was killed or not, and I've been hear…'

Pete was on the point of telling Dunny about the noises through his wall, but his friend interrupted him.

'Yeah, yeah, yeah, it's weird about Beth, and it's pretty spooky, but millions of things like that have happened in Clydebank because of the Blitz. Let's go and bounce.'

Dunny pushed through the hedge into his own garden expecting Pete to follow. He continued speaking as he climbed on to the trampoline and began to jump.

'I know loads of stories about people appearing or doing things after they were supposed to have been killed.'

He flopped on to his back and shouted towards Pete. 'I told you, something horrible happened to just about every family who lived in Clydebank during the Blitz. EVERY family.'

Dunny sat up and looked at Pete. 'My granny's twin brothers were killed when they ran back into the close to find her teddy bear on the first night. It's their anniversary too. Their mother stood screaming with my granny in her arms, telling them to come back, come back, but one of them shouted, "We'll just be a second, Ma, we canny leave her teddy behind", and the close was hit just as he was speaking.'

Dunny paused, suddenly solemn, looking into the distance, 'M'gran said the twins looked after her every minute of her life after that and last year, just before she died, my mum wouldn't let me go into her room because gran said the twins were waiting by her bed to meet me.' Dunny rose to his feet and bounced gently,

'Wish I *had* met them. That would have been mega. I know loads of stories like that. Things happen. No big deal, 'specially at this time of year at the anniversary of the Blitz.'

Pete leaned his arms on the trampoline mat and watched Dunny bounce.

'All I knew about the war, till now,' he said, 'was that London was bombed and kids got sent away from the cities.'

'Ach, all the history books just talk about London, London, London,' said Dunny, bitterly. 'Haven't you heard about the Blitz in Coventry either?'

Pete shook his head.

'Wonder what it would be like to be evacuated?'

'You could be sent somewhere really horrible, to people who didn't want you, and starved you, and stole all your coupons. That happened, you know.' said Dunny.

'Or you could be sent somewhere really cool, like the seaside, or a farm, and get spoiled rotten.'

'My teacher said when some of the kids from the slums in Glasgow were evacuated, the people who took them in were pure shocked 'cause they were so dirty and smelly. Imagine having all these smelly wee kids runnin' all over your house?'

'They'd have had nits.'

'And you'd have to let them share your room.'

'And they might pee the bed.'

'And be dead cheeky and play with all your stuff.'

'But it'd be pretty bad to be away from your mum and dad, and be worrying about them stuck in the city where they might be bombed.'

Pete was thinking about Beth. He couldn't stop thinking about her, and the more he talked about the war with Dunny, the more he wanted to know if she had survived the Blitz or not.

Dunny was concentrating on his bouncing, however, and Pete climbed up beside him and bounced gingerly. He had to work hard to stay upright as Dunny's landings propelled him in all directions. He was still thinking. It seemed the only person who would be able to tell him about Beth was Mr Milligan. When would he be back? And would he have a clue what Pete was on about? Pete remembered that he wasn't the only person who wanted to talk to Mr Milligan.

There was that funny woman.

CHAPTER TEN

'HE KNOWS what happened to her,' whispered Pete to himself. He stopped bouncing, and climbed down from the trampoline.

'Where you off to?' asked Dunny in mid-somersault.

'Better see if Mum and Dad need me to do anything,' said Pete.

This wasn't true, of course. He wanted to know when he would see Jamie Milligan again, but he wasn't going to tell Dunny just yet.

'Adios, amigo,' said Dunny.

Pete's parents were still arguing, but this time they were in the lounge.

'You'll just have to tell Milligan that you won't work overtime at weekends. Where would that leave me, stuck here with Jenny, knowing no one?'

'He's aware of that, Jo, but I need to put in as many hours as I can. I've been out of work for over a year. We need the money too, for goodness sakes.'

'It's all very well for him to tell you when to come in. He doesn't have a family and kids like us. I'll tell him our position when he comes back round in his big fancy car. Don't you worry.'

Pete had edged into the lounge unseen. His parents were squared up to each other in the centre of the room. They were both yelling although their faces were inches apart.

'What?' Mrs Smeaton barked at Pete when she caught sight

of him. 'Can't you give your father and me two minutes to have an adult conversation?'

'Huh! Conversation: more like a world title fight,' Pete snapped back.

There was no point in asking when Mr Milligan was coming back round at the moment. That would be like a red rag to his mother's wrath. Pete withdrew and climbed the stairs to his bedroom sighing heavily. He would never get married, he decided.

'And don't you *dare* suggest that I start going to coffee mornings to meet people,' Pete heard his mother shriek as he reached his room and closed the door behind him.

He sank down on his bed and put his hands over his face, sliding them round to cover his ears when he realised he could still hear his parents arguing.

He jerked up straight a moment later as the wall between his room and Beth's old bedroom gave a shudder as though someone had kicked it or shoved something hard up against it. Pete stared at the wall as though he expected it to move.

'Mummy!' yelled a girl's voice as clear as could be, 'Is my trunk under the stairs?'

'In the cubby hole,' came a distant female voice. 'I'm just running next door to see if Mary'll mind you tonight while I'm in surgery. See if you can find the trunk yourself.'

A door slammed, and Pete heard the girl – Beth, he presumed – move about through the wall. She was humming tunelessly. Then she left her room. Pete heard a door squeak followed by swift footsteps which retreated along the corresponding corridor leading to the top of the stairs in the other house.

Quickly Pete left his own room, ran along his own corridor and down his stairs. He wanted to keep up with Beth and mirror her movements. He shivered as Beth's hand brushed her wall, as though it had run along his arm. He knew that only a thin layer of lathe and plaster separated them. At the bottom of his stairs Pete lost her; her footsteps had died away.

He paused listening, trying to pick up Beth's trail above the noise of his parents' continuing argument.

'Yesss.'

There was the sound of someone bumping things together and sliding objects over a floor.

'She's gone under her stairs,' whispered Pete, 'We must have a cupboard there too.'

A brass handle allowed Pete into the space under his stairs. He hadn't found this cupboard yet. It was much larger in there than Pete had expected. Lofty at the entrance where the stairs were at their highest, getting progressively lower as the stair descended above him. Eventually there was no more than crouching space at the back.

Pete's cupboard was empty, long cleared of the domestic paraphernalia that normally accumulates in such a glory hole. On one shelf sat a few candles stumps, and on the floor by the door, lay a couple of old paint tins. It was pitch black at the back of the cupboard and the bareness and darkness seemed to emphasise the bumping and thumping from the cupboard directly through the wall.

Pete found a light switch but the bulb over the door didn't come on when he depressed it. He could just make out a trapdoor in the centre of the floor which must have led to the solum under the house. Pete moved in and stood over this trapdoor, feeling a chill draught blowing up his trouser legs. He squinted to see what might be further back, his body blocking all the light from his hallway. Stretching his arms instinctively before him to avoid bumping into anything, Pete moved further into the darkness until his hands struck stone.

It was completely dark, and Pete was crouched low as he groped around awkwardly. He seemed to have travelled sideways and beyond the lowest descender on his staircase. His left hand touched the wall which joined his house to Beth's. Here he could almost stand up comfortably again.

He could still hear the clatter of a search through the wall, but it seemed a little further back from where Pete now stood.

'I've gone past her,' Pete whispered to himself, 'She's behind me now.'

As he made to move back through the cupboard a cobweb – or something that felt like a cobweb – brushed his face. Pete yelped in panic, and started to thrash around, desperately swiping his hands over his hair and face, saying, 'Get away, get away. GET AWAY!'

His voice sounded like someone else's as it ricocheted off the stone which surrounded him on all sides. His movements disturbed damp and noisome smells which had probably slept undisturbed in this part of the cupboard for years.

In his fear and claustrophobia Pete did not realise that the bumping noises through the wall had ceased until through his own rapid breathing Pete heard Beth call uncertainly, 'Jamie? Is that you?'

Pete stopped writhing, held his breath, and listened. He was pressed up against the stone wall at the back of the cupboard trying not to sit on the floor which he imagined was covered in scuttling spiders.

His breath came so harsh in the empty space around him that Beth Winters must have heard it too, for she called out in a more anxious tone, 'Jamie? It is you, isn't it? Does your mummy know you're in there?'

'Jamie?'

'Are you stuck?'

Beth was alarmed. Pete could *hear* her worried breathing through the wall, and he knew that she was listening for tiny sounds on his side just as he was doing. He tried to stand up straight so that he could turn around and shout something through to Beth. But he stood up too quickly, and his head went all woozy.

Everything swam as Pete stuck out his hand to stop himself from losing balance. His body had already given an involuntary lurch forward, and he felt himself falling forwards.

'I'm going to faint,' he thought, as space seemed to part in front of him. Then Pete realised that his head was clear. And the hand which he had reached out to steady himself had pushed open a small door in the wall of the cupboard.

'Crikey Mikey!' exclaimed Pete in a loud voice. He had lurched into the space beyond the door and had not yet managed to stand up, which was just as well, for he would not have been able to do so.

He had fallen into a narrow brick tunnel, no more than one and a half metres long and less than a metre high. Pete had entered this space with such force as he lost his balance that he was half way through. He was able to examine the tunnel because light was seeping through the cracks of a doorway at the other end, and from this doorway, Pete could hear very clearly indeed the anxious voice of Beth Winters.

'Jamie! How did you get in there all by yourself? Hold on a minute. Don't you cry now.'

There was the sound of objects – metal, wood, boxes – being shoved aside, and of someone coming nearer. Pete, who was now splayed horizontally in the narrow tunnel, was dazzled as the low door opened and bright yellow light hit him full in the face.

He blinked into the startled blue eyes of the girl who had flicked his cheek with her plait at the entrance to the air raid shelter.

Beth.

CHAPTER ELEVEN

'YOU'RE NOT Jamie,' said Beth suspiciously, about to close the door on Pete. 'What are you doing here? How did you get into Mrs Milligan's house?'

Quickly, she glanced behind her as though she was planning to make a dash for it. Pete saw she was frightened although she was trying not to show it.

He was equally alarmed, and as he raised himself on his elbows, could feel his hands trembling. There was a weakness in the pit of his stomach. But he did not want Beth to leave.

'A... are you Beth?' he asked, immediately thinking how stupid the question was. He hoped he sounded friendly.

'What's it to you if I am?' Beth replied with some hostility, taken aback. 'How d'you know my name?'

'Saw your drawings, down the shelter. They're good. You signed them.'

Pete noticed a little smile play on Beth's lips.

'Ta,' she said immodestly, flicking back her hair. 'Want to be an artist when I grow up. Though I might still be a lady doctor, like mummy.'

Pete began to wriggle forward in the tunnel towards Beth, encouraged by the friendliness she had shown him so far. But she was having none of it.

'Hold it, you. You're not getting in here. Don't know who you are. You haven't told me what you're doing in the Milligan's house. And where's Jamie?'

Pete propped himself up on his elbows again, and looked at Beth.

'M'name's Pete Smeaton, and I've just moved in here. Last night. My dad's got a new job and we've come to live in Clydebank.'

'Ahhh.' Beth nodded her head wisely, seemingly satisfied with Pete's explanation. Her eyes lit up.

'You're an evacuee.' Beth thought for a moment, then frowned. 'Auntie Mary didn't say anything about you coming here. You come from England, don't you?'

'London,' nodded Pete.

Beth was puzzled, 'Why'd they send you up here? They're sending *me* away. And you say your dad's with you too?'

'And my mum,' said Pete.

'And your mum,' echoed Beth. She looked at Pete in

wretched disbelief.

'Your mother's with you. That's not fair.' Her voice seemed strained. Then, to Pete's horror – and embarrassment – Beth sank to the floor and began sobbing.

Pete could only watch helplessly from the tunnel, toying with the idea of crawling backwards until the tears had stopped, but then he thought better of it and took his chance to wriggle clumsily through the little tunnel to join Beth. He couldn't think of a single thing to or say as he watched this girl sobbing before him. He didn't know anything about girls and none of the boys he knew ever cried these days – not in public anyway – unless it involved a football international. Beth's crying was different from anything Jenny had produced so far, and this wasn't the way his mother cried. Great wracking sobs seemed to well from Beth's very soul. She was trying to speak too:

'I don't want to leave without Mummy and Daddy. They said they'll come but I'm afraid they're going to get blown up when I'm not here. How would you like it? Eh?'

She glared accusingly at Pete through her tears.

Then she gulped and smeared her hands over her wet cheeks, leaving them streaked with dirt. She wiped her nose on her sleeve and snuffled. Her shoulders juddered in misery.

Awkwardly Pete crouched down beside Beth and tentatively patted her shoulder.

'Hey,' he said. 'I'm sorry. Please don't cry. You're gonna make me cry, too if you don't stop.'

Pete was only half joking. He could feel his throat tight as he watched Beth, knowing exactly how miserable he would feel in the same situation. Beth's behaviour was making him feel like he did when his mum and dad were arguing and Jenny wouldn't stop screaming and he was worried about what his mum was going to do next.

He tried to change the subject.

'Hey. Listen, Beth. Don't cry. D'you want to know something amazing?'

'Like what?' said Beth, sinking her face into her hands and blurting through her tears. 'You've just killed Hitler and been made Prime Minister, and we're all going to get free chocolate?'

'Beth, listen to me. You know how I've moved into the Milligan's house, right?'

Beth managed a weak nod.

'So?'

'Well, I'm not an evacuee at all. Like what you mean. I've moved in more than sixty years after you were here. I'm from the 21st century.'

Beth heard the last bit all right. It sounded impressive, even to Pete himself. She stopped crying mid-sob and looked at Pete with new eyes. Taking in his clothes. Looking him up and down. Jeans. Sweatshirt. Trainers.

She frowned. Then she stood and looked down at herself, at her woollen jumper, her black-watch tartan kilt and thick knitted socks.

'If that's true, what you're saying, that I come from the past, then that means... it means,' she said in a small, uncertain voice, 'that I'm ...'

'A ghost?' interrupted Pete. 'I've been thinking that, but you don't look like a ghost to me even though your clothes are pretty old-fashioned.'

They stared at each other in silence. Pete wondered what Beth was thinking. He didn't think *he* would be too chuffed if someone told him he might be a ghost, especially when he felt totally alive.

Beth broke the silence.

'Wonder if I died in an air raid,' she said indifferently.

She smiled then. 'That would mean I didn't go away after all.'

'I don't know what happened to you, Beth,' Pete said, 'or how we've managed to meet up like this, but you don't seem very ghostly just now. I mean you're totally real. Look!' He squeezed her arm. 'I can touch you, and my hand doesn't pass through you. And I bet this hurts.' He squeezed harder.

'Ouch!' Beth flinched and pulled away. 'That was sore, you.'

'Am I scary? Do I give you the creeps?' asked Beth, crossing her eyes and trying – unsuccessfully – to make a grotesque face.

'Nah,' Pete laughed, 'you're just normal. Apart from the kilt. That *is* scary. You're not like any ghosts I've seen on TV.'

Beth was holding out the sides of her kilt with a wounded expression on her face.

'Seen on what?'

'Television. I've seen hundreds of ghosts on television.'

'I think I've heard of that,' said Beth. 'You could get it in America before the war started. They say it'll come to Scotland too one day and then you can watch pictures at home instead of going to the cinema.'

'Yeah,' said Pete, nonchalantly. 'We've got videos and DVDs. We watch films on TV. Had them for ages. Well, since I was born anyway.'

'That must be great,' said Beth. She sighed, 'But I still think going, actually going, to the cinema's better. It's like magic.'

'Oh, I go to the cinema, too,' said Pete. 'With Dad, usually.'

'Every week?' asked Beth.

'No way. Only when there's a big blockbuster, or it's someone's birthday or something. Mum says it's a ripoff once you've bought drinks and popcorn.'

'Oh, that's a shame. I go every week, sometimes twice. Every Saturday morning. Me and my friends. The ones that haven't gone away or been…'

Pete noticed Beth's lip trembling and interrupted quickly,

'You're lucky. I have to swim every Saturday morning.' Then Pete remembered, 'Well, I mean I used to, till I came here to live.'

'Funny, isn't it,' said Beth. 'You've just come, and I'm

about to leave.' She definitely sounded as though she would cry again.

'I'm being evacuated tomorrow morning. Just me and nobody else. I'm going away up North to live with my Aunt Katy in Beauly till the air raids stop and someone kills Hitler.'

''S that why you keep crying? Because you're leaving?' asked Pete. He was going to add that the war finished in 1945 and you won but decided against it.

Beth nodded, sniffing again. Tears were not far away.

'I can hear you,' said Pete, quickly. 'That's how I knew who you were. I can hear you through my bedroom wall. I can hear you crying and talking to someone, and playing the recorder. But I don't understand how this all happens in my time, when I know your house was bomb...'

'D'you hear my Skye Boat Song?' interrupted Beth, brightening suddenly. 'I'm practising for a school concert, but,' her face crumpled just as suddenly, 'I won't be here to perform it.'

Pete could only watch helplessly once more while Beth sobbed. He was glad she interrupted him before he told her about her house being bombed. That piece of information wouldn't have gone down too well.

'Mummy sent me down here to get a trunk for my stuff,' sniffed Beth, wiping her nose on her hand this time. 'I know where everything's going except for this.' Beth handed Pete a brown shoebox.

'Look,' she said, sniffing, 'Mummy's packed things from home to take away with me. Go on, you can open it.'

Pete obeyed.

At the top of the box lay a red cotton napkin edged with gold thread. Folded inside was a small elephant, beautifully carved. Pete lifted it out and examined it.

'That's nice,' he said. 'Hope it's not ivory.'

'Course it's ivory, ye daftie,' said Beth. 'All the way from Africa. Wouldn't be much of a souvenir if it wasn't ivory, would it?'

Beth's tone was sarcastic.

'What d'you expect it to be made of? Bakelite?'

'You can't bring stuff like that into the country nowadays,' said Pete, gravely. 'Elephants are endangered and you're not supposed to kill them for their tusks. And it's cruel. You could go to prison for it, you know.'

Beth shrugged and tossed her plait disdainfully. 'Why don't you report me then? Get me locked up. At least that would keep me here, wouldn't it. If you don't like my elephant, look at my postcards instead. My Uncle Robert sends me them from all over the world. He's in intelligence you know.'

'Is he a spy?' asked Pete, 'Like Bond, James Bond?' He attempted his Sean Connery impersonation.

'Who?' asked Beth with a withering look that said 'you're sad'.

Pete blushed. 'Oh, never mind. Are these your parents?'

Beth nodded.

'That's my mummy and daddy on their wedding day. Mummy was a flapper. Look at her hair. It was bobbed short and she was the height of fashion back then. Now it's all curly, and she's got bangs. Oh, look, she's got an ivory cigarette holder, so maybe she should have been arrested too.'

Pete, ignoring Beth's sarcasm barely glanced at the fashionable woman in the exquisite beaded dress and long, swinging rope of pearls. He didn't like the sound of bangs; probably some horrible disease you got from smoking with an ivory cigarette holder. He pointed to the tall thin man beside her.

'Why's your dad got a stick?'

'Lost his foot in the Great War. In the trenches. Got an iron one now.'

'He was in the First World War?' exclaimed Pete. 'He must be ANCIENT.'

Beth nodded in agreement and let her fingernail run gently around the form of her parents.

'Forty-three. Much older than Mummy. But he was only

nineteen when he lost his leg. All his friends joined up together. He was the only one who came home. Now he can't be sent away to fight.'

'That's good then, isn't it, having him here? Most dads must be away fighting.'

Beth nodded.

'But he's busy all the time. He's a doctor in the Western Infirmary in Glasgow. Most nights he doesn't come home because he won't drive after the blackout.'

'So why are you going away if your mum and dad are here?'

Beth sighed. 'There's supposed to be more air strikes on the way. Last week Bessie and Anna in my class were killed. While they were in their beds. Mummy doesn't think it's safe here any more. She's going to join me as soon as she can, but she's as busy as Daddy. Her partner's away in the army and she's the only doctor about. She won't listen when I tell her I don't mind being here on my own when she's working. If there's trouble I can always run through to Auntie Mary.'

'Your mum doesn't leave you here on your own when she's at work, does she?' Pete asked with a mixture of shock and envy. His mother would never dream of leaving him in the house by himself.

'Auntie Mary – well she's not my real auntie, she's Mrs Milligan, my next-door neighbour – she's here. I just run through if there's a problem. Although,' Beth began to giggle, 'I prefer to stay in my own house. Wee Jamie Milligan's a right pest. He always wants to play hide and seek in the garden and I get fed up doing that after about a million hours. I end up scaring him so he'll go away. He stinks. He's always wetting his breeks and not telling anyone.'

Beth grinned, and then asked, 'What about you, Pete? You haven't told me much about yourself.'

Beth sat on an old packing case gently rocking back and forwards while Pete found himself telling her about why he had moved to Scotland, about his dad's new job and even about his mum being tired and sad these days. He told her about meeting Dunny, and using the air raid shelter, and Wee Stookie's accident.

'Oh yes, I saw that boy and I wrote my name on his plaster. Thought it was Jamie. They're quite alike. I've had a go on that trampoline when no one's about, you know. And played with all those horrible ugly men wearing ladies' bathers.'

'They're wrestling figures, actually,' laughed Pete. 'Dunny thought someone was mucking around with them. It was you.'

Pete was thinking about something else.

'Jamie Milligan. I know him now. He's not a wee boy any more. Must be in his sixties. He's my dad's new boss, and our new landlord, and he's a big smoothie.'

Pete straightened up and tried to do an impression of Mr Milligan.

'Hi. Jamie Milligan. I've got a big deep voice and I think I'm the biz. Everything OK with you folks. Any problems? Lovely to meet you, Pete? And who's this young lady, then?'

Beth squealed with laughter. 'That's not the Jamie I know. Always crying about something or other and having jobbies in his drawers.' Beth giggled and chewed on the end of her plait, 'And d'you know what?'

'What?' said Pete, looking at Beth who seemed to be puzzling something.

'Every time I ask him to help me, he won't come down.' Beth stood up and looked down at herself. She seemed as confused with what she had just said as Pete.

'Why won't he come and help me look?' Beth was staring at Pete now, her blue eyes solemn and pleading.

'Maybe you can help me. Will you?'

'What you talking ab…'

'Beth? Hel-loo!'

Somewhere in Beth's house a door slammed and a woman's voice called through the hallway.

'Beth, I've got twenty minutes to get your packing sorted.

Have you found the right trunk?'

'Mummy!' said Beth in alarm, 'you'll need to go. She'll never understand what you were doing here.'

'*I* don't understand what I'm doing here,' said Pete, 'and I haven't a clue why you're here.'

Beth wasn't listening. She had turned Pete around and was manhandling him back towards the tunnel that led to his own house. She pushed him and pushed him until his body was completely out of her side of the door, which she proceeded to close by turning round and dunting it shut with her kilted bottom.

Just as the tunnel door closed Pete heard Beth's mother in the cupboard,

'Find what you wanted, love? Oh, don't forget that shoebox.'

'Sure you'll help me later, Pete-Smeet?' Beth hissed, as the latch dropped and Pete was left in the narrow tunnel between the two houses.

CHAPTER TWELVE

PETE'S face was millimetres away from the door that Beth had closed on him. His hands, which bore the weight of his crouched form, dug uncomfortably into the loose clinker which paved the tunnel. Glancing down he noticed his knuckles white and alien-looking, lit up by a slip of light which seeped through the crack at the bottom of the link-door from Beth's side. In the very moment that he stared at his knuckles, the light went out, leaving him in total darkness.

With the darkness arrived a certainty that dropped like a sheet of steel: whoever had been on the other side of that door was now gone.

Pete tried the door. It would not budge. He tried pulling it towards him, and then he shoogled it hard backwards and forwards. It refused to yield in either direction.

'Beth?' he called, puzzled and frustrated. 'What's happening round here?'

Pete pressed his ear against the door. Listened. All he heard was emptiness. He knew there was no one there.

Kneeling back on his hunkers, Pete tried to sit up, banging his head on the low ceiling of the tunnel.

'Ouch'.

As he reached up to rub the tender spot on his head, Pete's hand brushed what felt like another cowbeb.

'AARGH.'

With every nerve-end jangling, Pete reversed out of the tunnel, and belted through the cupboard, flapping and brushing and wriggling all over like a boy possessed.

He was so busy giving himself little wipes, and swivelling about to make sure that there was nothing stuck to the backs of his legs, that he had trodden three times on Mr Milligan's feet before he noticed him standing at the cupboard entrance with Mr Smeaton.

'Watch where you're going, Pete,' said Mr Smeaton. He held Pete at arms length and barked irritably, 'Look at you, you're filthy. What on earth have you been doing in there?'

'Exploring the cupboard,' said Pete, crouching down and pointing to the back of it. 'It's really deep, Dad, and it leads through to next door.'

'There is no next door, son. How many times do I have to tell you.' Pete knew his father was angry with him. He sounded as though he was speaking through gritted teeth. Turning to Mr Milligan, who had said nothing so far, he said breezily, 'Overactive imagination, this boy of mine. First it was crying through the wall. Now it's tunnels through the wall.' He turned to Pete. 'I'll see Jamie out, then you can show me what you're on about.'

'This young man's right, you know, Steve,' said Mr

Milligan, cutting Mr Smeaton short and giving Pete a meaningful look as he sidled past him into the cupboard. He had to stoop a little.

'There *is* a way through here into the house next door. At least there was when I was a lad, and before the Winters' side was bombed. Used to scare myself silly coming down here and opening that door at the back. Look. There was a wee tunnel that joined the two houses in there. No idea why it was built like that. I've never actually been through it. Too frightened.'

There was a silence. Pete thought Mr Milligan's last statement sounded like an admission. His back was to Pete and Mr Smeaton. He crouched down, and shuffled towards the door at the back of the tunnel. His greatcoat swept the dirty floor, but he didn't seem to notice. When he spoke his booming voice filled the cupboard, sending shivers down Pete's spine.

'Beth, the girl who lived next door, had me convinced that a goblin lived in there. Said it would eat me up if I crawled through. C'mere,' he steered Pete alongside him so that they both crouched before the open tunnel door.

'Feel that draught? Put your hand up against the door.'

Pete felt cold air whistle against his fingers.

'It was even draughtier when I was a boy because the other side was an open space, well ventilated. Now it's blocked with rubble and masonry.'

Mr Milligan chortled to himself. 'If I was feeling very brave I used to stand just in the doorway – no further mind – and I would open my mouth so I could feel the draught making my teeth hurt. That was until Beth told me the draught was really the goblin's breath. "Smell it, Jamie?" She used to say "Can you smell it? If you can smell it, then it can smell you." There was a horrible foosty smell down here right enough. Beth told me it was the stink of the wee boy burps from the goblin's stomach.'

Mr Milligan gave a pretend shudder.

'I was terrified to come down here after Beth told me that story. She had me waking up in the night.'

'Once d'you know what she did? She asked my mother if she could look after me, but she made me come down here by myself and wait for her. Then she went over to her side of the tunnel and growled at me in a horrible voice. I can still remember the fright. I screamed for about an hour. Wouldn't come down here again.'

Pete considered asking Mr Milligan if he'd wet himself in fright, but didn't think his dad would let him get away with that one.

Pete and the two men came out into the hallway. Mrs Smeaton poked her head out of the kitchen and called, 'Steve. Your mother on the 'phone.'

'Pete can see me out, Steve. Never keep your mother waiting. Catch you later.' said Mr Milligan, already striding towards the front door, steering Pete before him. ''Bye, Jo.'

Pete felt that Mr Milligan was escorting him deliberately to the door. A host of unanswered questions hung in the air between them. Pete knew that in a moment Mr Milligan would be gone, and there was still something he had to know about Beth Winters. Although he feared the answer he might hear, he took a deep breath and blurted, 'That girl, Beth. Was she in her house when it was bombed?'

Pete felt his shoulders tense as he awaited the answer.

Mr Milligan opened the front door. He steered Pete outside with him and closed it over behind them. He shook his head.

'No, no. She was in the air raid shelter with me and my mother. We had to stay in there all that night. Listening to the bombs falling. The doodlebugs. The explosions. I can still remember being terrified though I didn't really understand what was going on. My mother has talked about it so often, that I can, you know, remember bits. We came out at dawn and the Winters' house was totally destroyed. Right down to the foundations. That tunnel we were talking about on her side was full of rubble.'

Mr Milligan chuckled, 'I can even remember thinking thank goodness the goblin must be dead.'

'But none of the family were hurt?' Pete urged, looking searchingly at Mr Milligan.

Mr Milligan started to say something, then checked himself. He examined his shoes and said quietly, 'Beth was all right. She left the next morning.' He went on, 'All her belongings were lost in the explosion. She went with absolutely nothing. My mother was awfully upset about that.'

'So she never took that shoebox her mum had packed for her?'

Mr Milligan swung round and faced Pete.

'What?' he asked in a shocked voice. He was trembling. 'What did you say?'

'The box of stuff her mum made up for her; an elephant, a napkin, pictures and stuff.'

'How on earth do you know about that, son?' Mr Milligan walked away from Pete and leaned on the door of his car, gripping the roof sill until his knuckles showed white. He seemed miles away. Finally, he rested his chin on his elbow, masking his mouth with his hand, staring into the distance towards the ruin of the Winters' old house. Then he closed his eyes, and Pete was sure that he heard him say 'I should have helped her', but his hand was over his mouth, making his utterance indistinct.

Suddenly he opened his eyes, drew himself up to his full height and said in a normal voice, 'Well, Pete, before I tell you any more, I'd like to speak to my mother. And I'm late for her already.'

Pete stepped back to let Mr Milligan into his car. As he was closing the door, Pete blurted, 'So what about Beth's mum and dad? Were they all right? And if Beth was all right, how come I hear her through my wall when there isn't even a house there?'

Mr Milligan, who had been about to put his key in the

ignition, let his hand drop heavily into his lap. Slowly he turned to Pete, who was still talking.

'I want to know what happened to Beth, and her parents.'

'Yes, yes, yes, of course you do. You say you can definitely hear her through the wall?'

'Yes. I hear her crying because she doesn't want to leave her mother, and I can hear them talking. And there are footsteps.'

'That's right. Clicking footsteps, along the corridor.'

Mr Milligan had interrupted Pete and they stared wide-eyed at each other, caught up in the extraordinary recollection of their shared experience.

'And,' Pete went on, 'I've heard her playing that instrument thingy, the...'

'Recorder. She plays *The Skye Boat Song*. Terrible at it. She used to bring it down to the shelter sometimes, and when she was scared the notes came out all wobbly. Drove us all mad. Hate that tune.'

The far-away look returned and Mr Milligan placed both hands on the steering wheel of his car and closed his eyes.

'I can remember sitting on my mother's lap down in that shelter late at night and watching Beth. I used to pretend she was my big sister. She couldn't keep still. We used to look after her a lot, because her mum was so busy with casualties of the air raids. Beth hated being down there when her mum was outside. No wonder she tried to keep her mind off things with her recorder and her diary.'

'And her drawings,' interrupted Pete.

Mr Milligan whistled.

'You know about them too then, do you? My mother didn't like to see her scribbling on the walls like that but she let her do it. Probably to keep me quiet.'

'I've seen her down there too, Mr Milligan,' said Pete, excitedly. 'Today. She was in the shelter, writing on the walls again. And she signed a plaster on the boy next door's arm.'

Mr Milligan shook his head sadly and sighed.

'That'll be the Wee Stookie fellow. Took him up to the hospital couple of years back when he swallowed toilet cleaner. Thought I was his dad. You know, Pete, I thought she'd gone from here and found her peace. Thought she'd... well given up, I suppose. It's years and years since there's been any sign of her. I wonder why she's come back again this year?'

He turned to Pete. 'When I was growing up after the war, I heard her, too, just as you described, through the bedroom wall.'

'Wow,' said Pete. 'Weren't you scared?'

Mr Milligan shrugged.

'I was only four or five when it started, and I didn't bother about it too much at first. It wasn't – y'know threatening, or evil, or anything like that. Just a bit strange.'

Pete nodded in understanding.

'But when I went to school and told friends about it, they tried to scare me stupid telling me that I was hearing a ghost, and that my house was haunted. Lots of people were hearing, y'know, family they'd lost during the war. My story wasn't that unusual. I knew she couldn't be a ghost because she was still alive. I suppose I tried to ignore it.'

'So it bothered you?' asked Pete.

'Well, to tell you the truth, it did a bit when I was your age,' said Mr Milligan. 'I didn't want to sleep in my room – your room – any more, and I wouldn't go down to the air-raid shelter to play. I used to bump into her down there occasionally, you see, just like you said you did. She'd brush past me, and I'd run a mile.'

'Wow!' said Pete.

'Anyway, for years it all stopped. Not a sound or a sign of Beth. I forgot all about it, to be honest. By the time I was a teenager – this was the fifties remember – I was too busy playing my rock'n'roll records and worrying about girls to notice anything through the walls.'

'Cool. You were around in the fifties. Did you like Elvis

and Buddy?' Pete was becoming more and more impressed by Mr Milligan.

'Did I like them? Did I like them?' repeated Mr Milligan. He seemed relieved to change the subject. 'When I was fifteen I was saving up to go and live in Memphis, Tennessee. I had two jobs to pay for all the records and clothes I bought. Used to get stuff sent over from America. Kept it all, of course. It's worth a small fortune today. Show you sometime. But that's another story.'

Mr Milligan glanced at his watch.

'Look. Must go. We'll talk later.'

Mr Milligan prepared to drive away. Pete realised that he still did not know the most important facts about Beth and her parents.

'Mr Milligan.' He tapped on the car window, 'Please tell me, did Beth survive the war? And what about her parents?'

'Pete,' said Mr Milligan, winding down his window. 'I'm late for my mother. She'll miss her tea if I don't go now. If she's good today – she's a bit wandered, you see – I'll try and get her round here to talk to you. *She'll* tell you all you need to know.'

'Can't I just come with you and meet her now?' Pete was suddenly desperate to piece together Beth's story.

'No point, till I see how she is. Sometimes she can't remember who I am never mind what happened sixty years ago. But I promise to speak to her and get back to you.'

Pete stared after Mr Milligan's car and wondered what he was going to find out about Beth. He was in deep thought when a voice beside him said, 'Excuse me.'

The shock made Pete jump so vigorously that he went over on his ankle when he landed.

'Ouch!' he exclaimed crossly, rubbing the tender spot.

He looked up to see the woman in the bright clothes.

'Are you all right?' she asked, reaching out her hand as though to touch Pete on the shoulder. Her blue eyes were pale and anxious.

Pete recoiled from her, remembering his mother's instructions should he see this woman again.

'I'll get my mum,' he said, moving as fast as he could hobble up his front steps.

The woman made no attempt to follow but called after him with that funny voice of hers, 'No! NO! Just wondered if you'd found my box yet. Don't disturb anybody.'

'Hang on,' said Pete, 'I'll get mum.'

He disappeared into the house and when he returned moments later with his mother and father, his street was deserted once more.

'She's gone,' said Pete in frustration. 'That's the third time she's done that.'

'Well, if she comes round here again, we'll definitely get the police,' said Mrs Smeaton. 'Why would she disappear when you go to get an adult? Check and see if she's gone round to the ruined side, Steve. I don't like the idea of someone wandering around talking to the kids.'

'She's not scary,' said Pete. 'She's looking for something.' He remembered, 'And she's looking for Jamie. JAMIE. That must be Mr Milligan. She talks weird.'

'Everybody talks weird up here as far as I'm concerned,' said Mrs Smeaton. 'Maybe she's his wife and he's late for his tea.' She grinned and added, 'Seriously, Pete, I don't care how soft someone looks; you just don't get into conversations with strangers.'

'I was talking to Mr Milligan for ages and he's a stranger,' said Pete huffily. He was sure this woman had been harmless.

'Yes. What exactly were you two discussing?' Mr Smeaton wanted to know. 'Hope you weren't making a nuisance of yourself.'

'Nah,' said Pete, 'as if. We were discussing local history, actually.'

His father groaned. 'That means you *were* being a pest. No doubt asking him about crying children and what happened during the war. Please remember that I'm trying to create a good impression with Milligan. If you keep annoying him he'll get fed up with the lot of us, and I don't want to lose this job.'

Pete was indignant. 'He was telling *me* stuff, actually. And I wasn't annoying him. He's going to come back to see me with his mother so she can tell me the whole story of this house. And he wants to show me all his rock'n'roll collection.'

'Well don't be too disappointed if you find he's just saying that,' said Mr Smeaton. 'He's got far too much on his plate to worry about the past. And so have I as a matter of fact.'

Mr Smeaton locked himself away in the lounge with his paperwork while Mrs Smeaton, taking advantage of Jenny having a sleep, took the car and went off to do some more late-night shopping.

Pete was left to his own devices, and decided to go and see Dunny.

'You must be psychic,' he said. Dunny was thrashing his way through Pete's garden towards the house.

'You need a mega-lawnmower for this place,' said Dunny. I'd lend you my dad's but he's dead funny about his garden tools. Keeps them all polished up and locked away.'

The boys wandered down the garden. It was late afternoon, and a wind had got up. The long grasses and weeds whistled and rustled as they blew around the boys' legs.

'Cold up here in Scotland,' said Pete, zipping up his fleece and trying to huddle his neck down into the collar. 'London's warmer.'

'We're just tough up here, that's all, and you're a big wumman's blouse if you think this is cold. Just you wait till the winter sets in laddie, and the crops fail.'

The boys laughed as they thrashed through Pete's garden to the air raid shelter. They hesitated outside.

'Got your torch?' asked Dunny.

'Left it there,' said Pete jerking his thumb towards the

shelter. For some reason he was reluctant to go inside.

'You don't want to go in there just now, do you?' asked Dunny without enthusiasm, echoing Pete's thoughts. 'We'll hardly be able to see anything, and it's pretty creepy when it's dull like this. Let's go to my house and watch a wrestling video or something.'

Pete was disturbed by the gloomy shelter. He didn't want to go in, but he didn't want to leave either. Slowly he made himself push open the creaky door to see what it was like inside. The interior was really dark and grey, much darker than outside. He blinked. When his eyes had adjusted to the gloom, Pete saw the outline of a figure seated on the bench directly opposite him.

Pete inhaled with a gasp, his throat producing an involuntary rasp, which made the seated shape glance up suddenly.

Beth Winters' eyes met Pete's through the gloom and she held him in an unblinking stare. She gave no sign that she recognised Pete, or indeed that she was surprised to see him so soon after their last meeting. She merely lowered her head and resumed writing in the notebook on her lap.

Pete withdrew from the shelter and spluttered, 'Dunny, she's in there, sitting in the dark. She's writing.'

Pete's voice was tinged with fear, and it affected Dunny.

With eyes like saucers he whispered, 'There can't be anyone in there writing, dumbo. It's too dark.'

'See for yourself. It's her.'

Pete grabbed Dunny's sleeve and yanked him so hard towards the door that Dunny stumbled.

'No way I'm going in there,' he hissed so viciously, as he released his arm from Pete's grasp, that a shiver ran all the way down Pete's spine.

'Look, just see if she's there,' said Pete. 'I'll open the door and you look in. Go on, she won't bite you.'

Pete pressed the flat of his hand against the shelter door and flung it wide open. Dunny stood beside him, feet rooted to the spot. Pete deliberately kept his eyes on the ground this time: he couldn't bring himself to look at where he thought he had seen Beth.

'Hey, there's my torch,' he said. It was just beyond the door. Pete lunged forward and grabbed it before the door closed.

The two boys faced each other at the entrance of the shelter.

'Couldn't see anything inside,' said Dunny. 'C'mon, let's go.'

'Let's check again with the torch, and then we'll go,' said Pete ignoring his friend. He sensed fear in Dunny's voice and wondered if he had seen Beth sitting in the shelter but was too scared to admit it, even to himself.

'Let's check once more with the torch. You push the door open, and I'll shine it in. Then we'll see her.'

'Only if we can go after that,' said Dunny, reluctantly. He placed his hand against the door, 'Let's do it.'

'Right.'

'NOW!' chorused the two boys, hoarsely.

The torchbeam penetrated the darkness in front of the boys, reaching all the way to the back wall of the shelter, where it formed a pool of yellow light on the spot where Pete thought he had seen Beth.

'No one, you spookmaster,' said Dunny, with undisguised relief. The door swung shut again. Pete kept the torch switched on and swung it into Dunny's white face.

'I saw her. I did,' he insisted.

'Look,' said Dunny, exasperated, 'There was no one there.'

'I'm going back in to check again,' insisted Pete, 'just to make sure.'

Dunny thought for a minute, glancing towards the door, then at Pete, then back to the door.

'Promise we can leave after that THIS TIME?'

Pete nodded, 'C'mon, it'll only take a second.'

'Right, after three,' said Dunny.

The boys counted together:

ONE

TWO

THREE

They thrust themselves through the door so hard that it banged against the wall inside and closed behind them. Both boys were breathing very hard and without realising it, clutching each other by the arm.

Pete swung his torch around an empty space.

'Total numpty,' said Dunny, through gritted teeth. 'No one. You're giving me the heebie-jeebies.'

'What is this?' said Pete, 'I swear I saw her.'

'Good for you. I'm off,' said Dunny. 'This place is giving me the willies. I'll be scared to come down during the day after this.'

He didn't move. He wasn't going anywhere without Pete.

'Coming,' said Pete absently, shining the torch around the shelter one more time.

'I'm sure I… must be seeing… Sorry Dunny… Hang on, what's that?'

There was something lying on the bench just where Pete thought he had seen Beth a few moments ago.

'What's this doing out?'

Angrily Dunny snatched up a hard backed notebook which was lying open and face down as though someone had just laid it aside for a moment.

'See that Wee Stookie. He's dead if he's been at my things.'

'I don't think it was him, Dunny,' said Pete. 'It's lying just where I thought I saw Beth, and I'm sure she was writing in it too.'

'You saw me wrapping this up and putting it away,' said Dunny, perplexed. 'I'm sure I put it in one of my boxes under the bench.'

Pete held the torch over the notebook while Dunny flicked through the pages. Pete recognised Beth's neat handwriting, punctuated here and there with her clever cartoons.

Dunny was skimming through the entries at the back of the notebook.

'Pete,' he said in a voice which carried eerily through the shelter, 'something weird. Loads of this stuff is new.'

He stared at Pete with wide eyes.

'I've read this notebook loads of times, but there's stuff here I've never seen before.'

CHAPTER THIRTEEN

PETE and Dunny lay on the trampoline and pored over Beth's notebook.

'See this,' said Dunny, 'I've never seen any of it before.'

Dunny turned to the first couple of pages and the boys studied the early entries. On the inside cover Beth had written:

Elizabeth Julia Winters
14 Cairns Road
Clydebank
Scotland
Great Britain
Europe
The World
The Universe

and underneath in dramatic black letters:

I solemnly swear to keep this journal up to date for the rest of my life.

Below this promise Beth had signed her name with a flourish in red ink. Same signature as that on Wee Stookie's plaster.

The first entry took up half a page:

Halloween Night, 31st October 1940.
Dressed up as a sailor for the Milligan's party. Lucky Hugh was going to the pictures with a girlfriend, because I borrowed all his things. Just a wee bit big!!! Didn't win anything. Daddy was Charlie Chaplin, as usual, and he didn't win. As usual. Mrs Milligan dressed Jamie up as Shirley Temple in a pink frilly dress, and she put ribbons in his hair. He pranced around thinking he was right cute, till he tripped up and tumbled into the basin we were using to dook for apples. Blubbed and blubbed because his ribbons were all wet.

The sirens went off in the middle of the party so we took the apples down and dooked in the shelter. Mummy was a witch – as usual – so she didn't win. I told her to try something different next year.

'Who's Shirley Temple?' asked Dunny.

Pete shrugged. 'Thought it was a pink drink with cherries in it.' All he could think about at the moment was Mr Milligan in a frilly dress and ribbons. There was a brilliant picture in his head.

'And who's this Hugh?' he wondered absently. He looked at the next entry.

'Not much written here, is there?'

8th November.

Saw Hugh off at Central Station in Glasgow. He's going to England and then back to sea. Aunt Katy came down from Beauly just to wave him off. Probably because she's his godmother. She gave him some money and a gold cross, and she sniffed ALL *the time. Hugh was dead quiet with everyone, but then some of his friends arrived and he turned all loud and cheery and acted daft. Two girls turned up too. They didn't seem to know anything about each other, and Hugh hardly said a word to them, because he was talking to me. Told me to send him some drawings. Promised not to come back till he sinks all Hitler's submarines.*

9th November.

Aunt Katy still here. Mummy keeps taking her into the front room so they can whisper things. Every time I keek round the door they start talking in big loud voices about rationing. Aunt Katy brought eggs from the farm. We had merangues tonight. DEEEE-LICIOUS*!!!!!!!*

Mummy told Aunt Katy saving up six eggs for my birthday cake and when she cracked the last one into the bowl it was rotten and the cake mixture was spoilt. Aunt Katy said bet you can smell rotten eggs every time you eat birthday cake for the rest of your life, and then she said, to me, that I'd be having fresh eggs till they were coming out my ears right now if she had her way, and Mummy sounded annoyed and said she hadn't ruled it out completely yet, and that I didn't know anything about it so leave it just now, Katy.

'Bet they were planning to send Beth away then. That's a few months before she left,' said Pete.

There were no more entries until December, and flicking through the notebook the boys saw that Beth had only written a few sparse lines here and there:

6th December.

Mummy had to go out to a man who had crashed into the baffle wall outside his close in the blackout. He had a few drinks inside him, his neighbour said, and must have forgotten the wall was there. Mummy said loads of people've knocked themselves out against these walls. And they're supposed to be for protection. This man was in a coma now, Mummy said. She was really quiet tonight.

8th December.

Letter from Hugh. His boat was topedoed last week but he got into the lifeboat in time. Won't be home for Christmas. Hate this war!

14th December.

School panto. Load of rubbish. The choir sang flat so Mrs Banks kept me back and said I was putting everyone off-key deliberately. Was not. Least I don't have a big jelly bottom and a moustache.

18th December.

All going to Aunt Katy's for Christmas. Mummy says we need country air and I might like to stay up there for a while until the war's over. I don't think so, I said, and she said, well, we'll see. Wish we could stay at home for the Milligan's Hogmanay Party, but Aunt Katy's will be fun too. Hope I remember this notebook.

'She didn't write anything for ages, if she did bring it,' said Dunny. 'There's nothing else till February.'

Someone sent me A VALENTINE. Yuk. If it was Micky Kelly I'll die. Anna said it was him because he's always staring at me with his mouth open and googly eyes. His breath stinks of kippers. Boys make me boke. I'll never get married or anything.

'She should be so lucky,' said Dunny. 'She wouldn't be saying that if she saw me. Look what she says here.'

19th February.

Got a Valentine from Hugh. It's all covered in rosebuds.

'That's sick, isn't it, getting a Valentine from your brother. Anyway, that's the last of the entries I've seen until these new ones.'

'Let's have a look at them, then,' said Pete. Nothing very exciting so far, is there? Kind of girly stuff.'

He turned a page. Dunny began to read aloud in a high girly voice:

10th March.

I've to write out 100 times I must bring my gas mask to school for it could save my life. Stupid old Jelly-Bum Banks.

The boys laughed at Dunny's voice, which was disturbingly high. He sucked in his cheeks and continued in the same voice:

11th March.

We were in the shelter for ages last night. I fell asleep and woke up all stiff and freezing. There were bombings and raids going on all the time. It was horrible. Daddy was in Glasgow working, but Mummy stayed with me in the shelter. I fell asleep but Mummy said she didn't. Jamie Milligan was sick in the bucket we have to pee in – again.

Dunny reverted to his own voice, 'None of this was here the last time I looked. Where did it come from?'

There were two entries on facing pages. The first was dated 11th March 1941.

'Let me read, this time,' said Pete. He spoke in his normal voice:

I'm going away in two days, after all. Aunt Katy'll meet me off the train at Inverness. I know they've been talking about it since before Christmas, but nobody bothered to ask me what I thought. And I think it stinks. Mummy can't even come. She's too busy here with all the people hurt. Last night two streets were hit and some of my class live there. Micky Kelly and Frances McGraw. I keep thinking about them, and I can hear their voices in my head, and when I shut my eyes Micky's smiling at me, and looking at me with his googly eyes. Mummy's keeping me off school, but I'll have to start a new one in Beauly next week. There'll only be about twelve children in the whole school and one teacher for all the different classes. It'll be horrible without Mummy and Daddy. Hugh won't know I'm going away. What if he writes and there's nobody here? I'm taking his Valentine card with me. And Micky's. Wish Hugh would come home. If he knew I was leaving he'd take me to the pictures and get me chocolate. When I think about leaving Mummy I get a horrible feeling inside me that makes me want to cry, but

when she talks to me I'm angry and nasty, and I try to hurt her feelings because she's making me go away. Going to pack. Stop writing
NOW.

Dunny closed the notebook and flopped over on to his back on the trampoline. Pete picked the book up and hugged it to his chest. The boys lay side-by-side and stared up in silence at the cloudy evening sky.

'Wonder if the sky looked the same in her time,' said Dunny.

'Course it did,' said Pete, 'It can't change. But you probably wouldn't have wanted to be out here staring at it with all those German war planes zooming above you.'

'Pretty exciting, eh, all that fightin',' said Dunny. 'Wish we could have a war.'

'Nah,' said Pete, holding up the notebook with outstretched arms. 'Look at what happens to people like us in wars. Supposing we became refugees kicked out of our houses, having to leave everything behind and walk all the way to another country. And being bombed, and tortured, and shot. That's what happens in wars these days. I think it must have been pretty scary in Beth's time too, especially during the Blitz. How would you like to have to get out of bed to run down to that shelter in the middle of the night and then just sit inside waiting, and listening while all those explosions went on and on around you, and you couldn't see what was happening. You just had to sit there hoping nothing hit.'

The boys were silent. Pete, eyes closed, visualised a sky full of hostile aircraft. He felt the prickle of fear in his scalp. He could hear his heart thumping in his chest. He was thinking about Beth.

'NYAAAACHCHCH!' said Dunny sending his arm up in the air like a plane and letting his fist crash down on to the notebook on Pete's stomach.

'Ooofff,' Pete shot up, winded.

'Nyeaw! Nyeaw ! Nyeaw!'

Dunny thumped the notebook again and again making the trampoline vibrate.

'Just think,' he said, excitedly, 'the sky all lit up with flames and shells exploding like giant fireworks and sirens screaming all around. Pure Ace, man.'

'Yeah, but we'd be down in that shelter praying that none of those fireworks landed on our house.'

'Or your head. BOOM! SPLAT!'

Pete shivered. Dunny's images were making him uneasy.

''S freezing. I'm going in. Mum'll be back now. Can I borrow this notebook to look at tonight?'

Dunny shrugged. ''Slong as I get it back. Or you're dead.' He began to bounce on the trampoline.

'You'll need to let me practice my front falls. Gotta be able to do loads of stunts to be a wrestler. Probably see you tomorrow?'

'See you,' said Pete, secretly delighted that he had a friend. 'Thanks for the notebook.'

Pete's parents were arguing again, this time over swatches of fabric. Pete managed to scoot past the lounge door before his mother spotted him and uttered the dreaded words: 'Come and tell us what one *you* like, Pete.'

From experience he knew he would innocently choose whatever his father liked, and his mother would go all moody on them both, and accuse them of ganging up on her.

Jenny must have been ruled out as a design consultant because she had been dumped in the hall in her car seat, facing a wall. Only a pathetic gurgle as Pete made for the stairs signalled her presence.

'Hiya, Jenny. Have they left you out here in the dark?' Pete whispered as he unclipped his sister and lifted her gently to his shoulder.

'Come up with me and look at this notebook,' he whispered in her tiny ear, 'Something very strange is going on around here and I think it's time you knew about it.'

Laying Jenny beside him on the floor where she could play with his fingers, Pete leaned against his bed and carefully read through Beth's notebook again.

Why do these new entries suddenly appear, he wondered? It was as if Beth was drawing attention to what happened.

'What d'you think Jenny? What's going on? There's nothing scary about Beth. You'd probably like her, even though she wears horrible woolly clothes. And d'you remember Mr Milligan with the big loud voice? Well he knows what's going on, but he won't tell me everything. I'm hearing noises through this wall, you know, but nobody lives there any more. Come and listen with me. We might hear something.'

Pete pressed his ear against his bedroom wall and listened. Gently he positioned Jenny's fluffy head so that her ear also touched the wall.

'Listen,' he whispered.

Jenny kept perfectly still at first, as though complying with Pete. Then she started to wriggle alarmingly and Pete had to tighten his hold to prevent her slipping from his arms.

Suddenly he felt his sister's tiny body stiffen, as her head turned in response to something which made Pete's heart leap into his mouth.

The unmistakable wail of a siren welled up through the wall. Pete no longer needed to press his head against it, for the sound, barely muffled, grew and grew, resonating through Pete's head and sending a vibration through his whole body. He shook his head vigorously as if to shake away the insistent tone, but instead it rose in pitch and volume. Jenny, still stiff, began to cry, the note of her distress less shrill than that of the siren sound. To this cacophony new sounds were added as thumpings and clatterings and crashings were heard through the relentless siren.

Things were being flung wildly about next door. Something struck the wall just where Pete stood. Its force was so hard that Pete automatically recoiled. Still the siren continued to drone with a horrible sense of urgency. Then Pete heard a woman shouting.

'Leave everything up there. Come down right now. *Right now*. Do you hear me?'.

Pete's first reaction was to think it was his own mother calling, and he gathered himself to move, but then a girl's voice shouted peevishly,

'I'm *coming*, but I can't see that box you gave me. Give me a minute will you.'

'Beth Winters, get yourself down here this instant. Do you hear me?'

The woman's voice was angry, almost a shriek. Pete recognised fear, too.

'Don't nag,' Beth screamed back in temper, the siren still wailing above her voice. Pete heard footsteps, first moving across Beth's bedroom and then clattering downstairs: THUMP, THUMP, THUMP.

Still the siren wailed. Jenny screamed.

Then suddenly the noise stopped and there was complete silence. Even Jenny paused for breath. The after-ring of the siren pulsed in Pete's ears.

At that same moment the electricity failed in Pete's bedroom.

The abrupt click into darkness, not to mention Pete's involuntary jerk of fear that almost pitched Jenny out of his arms sent her into a paroxysm of screaming. Pete, too stunned by everything that had happened in the past few minutes heard stumbling noises again, but this time they came from his own hallway.

'Pete, are you OK?' It was Mr Smeaton. There was the sound of him falling over something.

'Oh no,' Pete heard, 'I've kicked Jenny over. Jenny! Can't see a thing. She's not making a sound.'

Pete shuffled forwards towards the top of the stairs with Jenny screaming lustily in his arms.

'Dad, I've got her up here. She's OK. But I can't see to get down. Did you hear that noise?'

'I know, Pete. I can't believe the lungs she's got on her. Oooh, m'knee, ooh ahh.' Pete heard his father struggle at the bottom of the stairs, 'Don't move, son. I'll get her for you.'

'What's happened? Where's Pete? Who's got Jenny? Where's the circuit board in this place? I'll check for a fuse.'

Pete just made out the shadowy shape of his mother groping her way towards the front door. Obviously neither she nor Mr Smeaton had heard the siren.

'I can't make out a thing down here. Don't know where the main switch is,' she said, crouched over the electricity cupboard. 'Where's your torch, Steve?'

Pete jumped when his father spoke right beside him. He had climbed upstairs to retrieve the screaming Jenny.

'In the car. Don't touch anything till I get it in case you blow us all up.'

'Hardly likely when the power's off, dear,' said Mrs Smeaton sarcastically. 'But I do need the torch before I can do anything.'

'Dad, I've left the torch down in the shelter, I think. Dunny and I were using it today.'

'Well, Pete. You'll just need to go and get it now, won't you, son.' There was irritation in Mr Smeaton's voice. 'I hope you remember where you left it.'

'I-I don't want to go down there by myself in the dark,' said Pete.

'You should have thought about that when you didn't bother putting it back where you found it. It's no blooming darker down there than in here, is it? On you go, Pete. Hurry up. Jenny's going ballistic.'

Pete hesitated in the hallway, suddenly filled with dread. After what had just happened in his bedroom, he did not want to go down to the shelter on his own. However this was definitely not the moment to mention noises through the wall to his father again.

Fumbling his way through the hallway, he stumbled to his back door and let himself out into the garden. It seemed lighter outside than in the house and that made Pete feel slightly better. He could see the shape of the shelter silhouetted in the light of an almost full moon.

'Right. Go!' he said, and plunged his way though the unkempt grass. Chilly stalks stroked Pete's hands like cold, grasping fingers. He shivered, but kept on moving.

The door of the air raid shelter scraped the ground slowly as Pete swung it open and gazed inside. It was pitch black.

'Right,' Pete thought. 'Torch should be on the floor where we left it, right there.' With one large stride Pete lunged into the shelter still holding the door open with one hand, terrified to let it close behind him. He squatted down and with his free hand he patted the ground in a circle around the area where he was sure the torch should be.

Nothing.

He tried to pull the door back a bit further and, still crouched down, shuffled deeper into the dark shelter. His arms were at full stretch as he held open the door, and he barely kept his balance. He kept his head turned away from the interior of the shelter, in case he saw something there that he didn't want to see, and fixed his gaze towards the garden and his house beyond. The muscles in his thighs strained as he wobbled to keep his crouched position. He smacked the ground all round and let his hand sweep across lumps and bits of gravel and soft irregularities.

But there was no torch within the circumference of his search. He would have to let the door go and crawl around on his hands and knees towards the corners of the shelter where the torch may have rolled. Pete released his fingertips from the door, and shivered as it scraped shut enclosing him in total darkness.

Pete closed his eyes tightly, and with his hands, carried out a blind search of the shelter floor beginning in the corner nearest the door. He also ran a hand along each section of bench he passed, finding nothing. Blindly, he worked as swiftly as he had ever done anything in his life, accompanied only by the sound of his own shaky breath and the sweep of his hands and knees over the rough ground.

When he groped underneath the section of the bench where last he had seen Beth sitting and writing, he expected to feel the boxes of toys which Dunny stored there. The space was empty. Pete gulped and tried not to think why the boxes were no longer there. Even more swiftly he completed his search, sighing with relief when, torchless, his hand brushed the corrugated metal of the shelter door. He was quite prepared to face his father's anger rather than prolong his time in the dark, mysterious shelter.

'Not here,' Pete's whisper seemed to echo all around him. Then he remembered: he had used the torch on the trampoline to read Beth's notebook.

He was just about to get to his feet and stumble gratefully to the door, when, from the furthest corner of the shelter, Pete heard the sound of something moving as if it had been pushed. An object rolled across the floor and touched Pete's knee. Without opening his eyes, Pete picked up the torch.

His thumb found the on/off switch and he flicked it on and opened his eyes.

His vision was immediately flooded by the sensation of light, not bright light, but a steady orange glow. At first Pete could not distinguish anything but gradually details of his surroundings grew clear.

The shelter was transformed.

In the centre, inches from where Pete knelt, there burned a small brazier. Its searing heat was enough to make Pete rear back from it. The dim light it gave radiated through the shelter. A tin kettle stood by the brazier and beside it was piled a collection of cups and saucers, none of them matching. A stack of small boxes teetered by the door, a gas mask spilling from the open lid of the top box. On the bench near the door were stacked loosely-folded blankets and floral-patterned eiderdowns. There was a half-filled milk bottle balanced on a couple of suitcases in one corner.

Sweeping his gaze quickly round the shelter, Pete took in all these details. But it was the people in the shelter that he noticed more.

Facing him sat Beth Winters huddled in a blanket. Pete could see the outline of her knees drawn up close to her chin. Her head rested on her chest so that only the parting of her blond plaited hair was recognisable. Along from her sat a woman about his mother's age holding the hands of a toddler who leaned against her. This woman sang softly in a cracked whisper, swinging the toddler's hands in time:

> '*Clappa clappa handies, daddy's comin' home,*
> *Pennies in his pocket for Jamie alone.*'

'A-*dain*,' said the child, and the woman repeated the verse, more softly this time. As she sang she looked upwards towards the sky that she could not see. Pete thought her face looked sickly white.

There were others in the shelter. Four elderly people sat opposite the mother and child, huddled in coats watching the toddler blankly.

The air in the shelter felt stale to Pete, tinged with something vaguely unpleasant. There was an unmistakable atmosphere of tension. The dim, tired light from the brazier infused everything with a sickly yellow tinge.

No sooner had Pete taken stock of the scene before him than Beth gave a whimper and an almighty crash from somewhere very near shook the shelter. It was followed by several smaller explosions in rapid succession. She looked upwards with terror in her eyes and called out, 'Mummy, Daddy.'

Keeping hold of the toddler with one hand, his mother put her arm comfortingly around Beth.

'Shoosh, shoosh, darlin'. It's all right.'

The four older occupants of the shelter shuffled nearer the

younger group. None of them spoke. None of them needed to. Their fear and anticipation was palpable as they glanced upwards and round about them with strained, worried faces.

Another giant blast rocked the shelter shaking the walls and making the crockery rattle. A cup fell from the pile on to the floor and smashed. Little Jamie screamed. Pete knew this because his mouth was open and his face was crumpled up in misery, but any sound he made was rendered silent by the relentless bone-shaking bombardment that went on and on and on.

Pete was screaming too. At least his mouth was open and his throat strained in terror. Louder and louder, nearer and nearer landed danger, as though the little air-raid shelter was the only bullseye in the whole of the Blitz.

No one in the shelter seemed to notice Pete. They clustered together in one corner seeking comfort in each other.

And then it came.

The loudest, most deafening blast of all. And the closest. The very closest.

BOOM!!!!

And silence.

Pete, along with everyone else in the shelter pressed his hands to his ears to soothe the screaming after-ring of the attack. Through the clanging in his head, he heard Beth cry as she rose to her feet and rushed towards his crouching position near the door.

'That was here. That one was right here,' she was saying, as a momentary lull followed. Pete felt rather than heard the thud of tumbling masonry outside. And then the bombardment resumed. Closer and louder than ever.

This time the sense of terror in the shelter was even more palpable. And Beth could stand it no more. She yanked at the door shrieking above the attack outside, 'Mummy. I'm going to find Mummy.'

One of the men and Jamie's mother, with the sobbing

toddler holding on to her skirt, hurried to restrain Beth. Pete witnessed the tussle between them, horrified by the scene he had stumbled into. He watched Beth wrestle with the grown-ups at the door, fighting to escape the claustrophobia of the vulnerable shelter.

'Let… me… go!'

And as he watched, unsure if he was observed or not, her panic became his.

Blindly he forced himself between the struggling bodies and flung the door open, stumbling outside to face the bomb-filled night sky.

Except there were no bombs outside his shelter. And no one tried to stop him. The garden was silent and still and evening-fresh. Pete faced the ragged silhouette of his house and saw the figure of his father coming towards him in the darkness.

'Power's on, Pete. Get the torch, did you? Mr Milligan popped back in with his mother, and luckily he knew what to do with the switchboard.'

He put his arm round Pete's shoulders.

'I'll take the torch though, and keep it handy; apparently there's a weakness in the new circuit board, and we'll need to keep an eye on it. Hey, what's up, son, you're shaking like a jelly?'

They were inside now and Mr Smeaton looked harder at Pete.

'You're deadly white. Cold out here, right enough.'

Speechlessly Pete gave the torch to his father. He could hardly believe what had just happened to him in the shelter, and felt deeply shocked. Not only because he had somehow gone back in time to the past, but also because he realised that he had probably experienced the very blast which had destroyed Beth's home.

He stood at his back door looking towards the black shape of the shelter. Someone touched him gently on the shoulder, making him jump.

'Pete, this is my mother, Mary Milligan. I told her about our chat today, and she was desperate to meet you tonight.'

'Take me down to the shelter,' said a tiny, stooped woman squeezing past her son to grasp Pete's hand. 'Tonight of all nights I think I'd like to go down there. This is the night all us Bankies remember, you see.'

She took Pete's arm as they made their way through the garden.

'What time is it, Jamie?' asked Mrs Milligan. 'Is it nine?'

'Well after that now, mother,' said Mr Milligan.

'Nine o'clock, 13th March 1941 I came down here just like this, with Jamie here in my arms, and wee Beth.'

'Beth Winters.'

'You know her, of course,' said Mrs Milligan, matter of factly. 'Fine wee girl she was. That was her last night with us. Och, it was terrible, so it was. I wish we could have kept her here.'

Pete felt a cold chill spread over him as he recalled Beth's panic to escape the shelter and find her mother. Could he have been responsible for her fate? Maybe he could have prevented her from escaping. With sinking heart Pete dared ask the question he had wanted to ask ever since he had known of the existence of Beth Winters.

'Did Beth die here, in the bombings?'

Pete clenched his fists, dreading Mrs Milligan's answer.

'No, no, son,' said Mrs Milligan reassuringly, 'Jamie must have said. Beth wasn't killed, although it was a miracle none of us were.'

They had reached the shelter. Pete let Mr Milligan enter first with his mother. No one, Pete realised, had brought a torch, but that didn't seem to bother Mrs Milligan. She swung open the door and went inside. Pete entered last.

'Come and sit down, Pete, and we'll tell you what happened, and you can tell my mother about the noises through the wall,' said Mr Milligan.

'If only we had the wee brazier in here we'd be quite snug.

D'you remember, Jamie?' said Mrs Milligan her voice rising eerily through the darkness of the shelter.

'*I* do,' thought Pete, taking a seat on the bench beside the old lady. Now that he knew Beth had not died he no longer felt quite so afraid in the shelter.

CHAPTER FOURTEEN

MRS MILLIGAN began, 'We lived next door to the Winters for eighteen years. Maybe Jamie's told you that. They moved in when their son, Hugh, was just a baby. Archie, my eldest, was a fireman and ended up in the Navy alongside Hugh. They were great friends. Archie talked Hugh into enlisting in the Navy and not the Air Force. Luckily they both lived through the war, although they were torpedoed.'

'So Hugh Winters is still alive?' Pete interrupted. He was thinking of Beth's diary, and the Valentine.

'Became a doctor, like his mother and father,' said Mrs Milligan, 'Went down South. Hasn't been back here for years, though, has he Jamie? People lose touch. Archie hasn't heard from him for a long time.'

'They still send Christmas cards, mother,' said Mr Milligan. 'Both in their seventies now, Pete,' explained Mr Milligan, 'My mother talks as though they were still wee boys.'

'That's how I see them. I'm ninety three you know,' added Mrs Milligan proudly. Then she sighed and went on.

'Anyway, where was I?… Wee Beth became very close to our family. You were that fond of her, Jamie. "Me play Beth, mamma. Me play Beth." I can still hear your wee voice beggin' me a hundred times a day.'

'D'you mind mother,' said Mr Milligan with an

embarrassed cough, 'get on with the story before you catch your death down here.'

'Jean – Beth's mother, and myself were good friends. I used to mind Beth when Jean went back to work. We had rare times.'

'Until I came along,' said Mr Milligan.

'Had my hands full then,' said his mother. 'What a gurny wee thing you could be. Snivelling and crying if the wind changed. Beth had the magic touch, mind you. Just the sound of her voice would make you smile.'

Pete thought of Jenny turning her eyes towards him.

'When the war came Jean was called out at all times of the day and night to attend to casualties. So many stupid accidents because of the blackout. Cars couldn't use their headlights, and people walked into walls and fell down bomb-craters. And then there were the real emergencies. Whole families burned alive in their homes. Oil bombs. Terrible.'

Mrs Milligan tutted sadly, 'Jean Winters came home some nights and just took Beth into her arms and held her. You didn't need to ask. You knew it was a child.'

The old lady's voice faltered, and there was silence in the shelter.

'What about her dad? ' asked Pete in a small voice.

'Aidan, that was his name. Quiet fellow. Surgeon up in Glasgow. Spent most of the war in the hospital. Wouldn'ae drive at night during the blackout unless there was an emergency – he'd seen too many pointless accidents. Aidan had an iron leg; lost his on the Somme when he was a teenager. Gave him a lot of bother.'

'What happened to him, Mrs Milligan, and to Beth's mother?' urged Pete, 'They weren't with Beth when the house was bombed.'

'That night would have been Beth's last night at home until the war was over. Her mother had arranged for her to go up North.'

'I know,' said Pete.

Mrs Milligan, went on, 'Lots of people were evacuated during the war to less dangerous places than the cities.'

'I know,' said Pete, with a hint of impatience, 'we did that in school.'

'Well you'll know about the Phoney War in 1939?'

'That was when parents sent their children away and Hitler didn't do anything,' said Pete.

'That's right, Pete,' said Mr Milligan, 'although he was doing plenty to his own people nearer home. But you'll know that most of the evacuees drifted back to the cities again and a lot of them didn't fancy evacuating a second time.'

Mrs Milligan continued, 'Jean hadn't sent Beth away the first time, but by 1941 things were getting bad, and so Beth was all packed and ready to leave on the morning of the 14th.'

'I heard her doing her packing, talking to her mum through the wall,' Pete burst in eagerly.

'And playing yon song on the recorder.'

'*The Skye Boat Song*,' laughed Mr Milligan.

His mother laughed, 'That was her party piece, wee lamb. She used to practise it down here till we begged for mercy.'

'So she packed,' said Pete, keen to get back to the story, 'but did she go?'

'Well, that night, at nine, the Blitz began and lasted all through to the morning. Terrible, so it was.'

Pete thought about the siren in his bedroom – that had started around nine – and his strange experience in the shelter with Beth and the others when he had heard the bombs falling. He shivered. Mrs Milligan almost whispered.

'One of the worst nights of my life.' The old lady turned to her son. 'You still remember it too don't you, Jamie?'

Mr Milligan said 'Mmm. Vaguely. I was only three, but I do remember being closed in here for ages and feeling scared.'

'You've no idea what it was like to sit and wait for the next bomb to land. And to know, to KNOW that it was all our own people, our friends, our children taking the shells that missed us. That's a hard one to live with.'

Mrs Milligan's voice faltered. She sighed deeply and Pete heard her sniff.

'Tell him about Beth, Mother,' Mr Milligan's voice gently coaxed.

'Oh, aye, Beth. Well when the warning sounded she was packing, but she had to leave everything where it was. She was right sore about going away without her mother. Jean had promised to be with her as soon as she could, but she wasn't the kind of woman who could walk away from people who needed her. Anyway, when the siren went off, Jean ran down to the surgery, and I brought Beth to the shelter with me and Jamie. We were there all night. And the Glancys and the Lyons. All sitting out the night, waiting for something to land on us. But it didn't. We all got out the next morning in one piece, but my God, what those Germans had done to the place. All around as far as the eye could see, was destruction. They say that only a handful of properties were undamaged during that Blitz. Well, it didn'ae look like that to me. All around us everything looked to have collapsed, and I don't just mean buildings. That night and the next tore the heart and soul from Clydebank, and no one who was there will ever forget.'

'Beth, Mother,' whispered Mr Milligan, 'tell Pete about Beth.'

'When we left the shelter the next morning, there was Beth's home, gone, and our half left standing. I was almost ashamed to see it still there with so many other places ruined. We were all in shock at the sight, and desperate for news of the people we knew. The atmosphere about the place. Dreadful, it was. I remember Beth's father came to find her, and I swear he expected to find her dead. Told us of the churches and factories and tenements along the way from Glasgow that had been flattened to the ground. And the silence as people searched among the rubble looking for their own.

'Doctor Aidan took one look at where his home had stood,

and said "Right, M'lady", and whisked Beth off to the station. She was crying so sore, looking back at her house as she left. I'd have been more use to her, but I had my own problems that day. My husband – he was a warden – had been out all night and I was worried sick about him. Somebody came and told me he'd had a bad fall searching a building for survivors. I'd to leave Beth then, and go to my Paul.'

'And was he? Your husband, was he…?' Pete could scarcely ask.

'Och, he survived, and recovered. But he never worked again.'

'He died years ago, Pete, and was ill for a long time, but Dr Aidan was very good to him,' said Mr Milligan.

'So Beth,' Mrs Milligan interrupted, 'left that very day. She took nothing with her: only the clothes she stood up in. One of the neighbours gave her an old coat to wrap around her on the train. She was breaking her wee heart because she didn't get taking her Land Girl's outfit. But it was lost somewhere under all that rubble.'

'So she didn't have her special box, then?' asked Pete.

'That was hard for her, wasn't it, Mother?' said Mr Milligan.

'They salvaged nothing from that house. Beth was all for scrabbling through the rubble to find that box. But her father wouldn't let her near the place. It was all groaning and creaking and shifting. Horrible sounds coming from it. Like it was moaning in pain. Dr Aidan made Beth say her cheerios and took her off.'

Mrs Milligan clicked her tongue sadly.

'Was Beth's mum alright? I mean had she been hurt during the night?' asked Pete.

Mrs Milligan's voice was trembling as she answered. 'She was lucky that time. Her surgery was hit, right enough, but she was out attending the casualties. Beth got to say her goodbyes to her mother – at least there was that – and then her father packed her off to Beauly. Even stuck one of those big address labels round her neck in case she went missing on the way.'

'Must have been pretty bad, leaving your mum and dad like that, knowing how dangerous things were.' said Pete, thinking aloud.

'Yup,' said Mr Milligan. 'And of course the next night it all happened again.'

'The bombing you mean?'

'That's right. Fortunately, lots of people had the same idea as the Winters and got themselves, or at least their children, away from Clydebank. There were fewer casualties that night.'

Mrs Milligan spoke. 'But that was the night that Beth lost her mother.'

A cold shiver ran through Pete.

'No!' he cried. The words hit him like a stone.

'So sad,' said Mrs Milligan, 'her body was found a couple of streets away. Folk said she was nipping back to see if she could find yon box for Beth. She knew how much the wee things inside would have meant. Lovely woman. Not the only mother to die needlessly in that war. Aye, there were many more.'

Silently, Pete and the Milligans sat in the shelter, thinking their own thoughts.

If Beth wasn't the one who died here, Pete was wondering to himself, why did she keep appearing around the shelter?

As though he could read Pete's mind, Mr Milligan spoke through the darkness of the shelter.

'Thing is, Pete, every year, around this time when I was growing up, I used to hear voices through the wall, too… Just like you. It went on and on for twelve, thirteen years, always at the same time of year.'

'The anniversary of our terrible Blitz,' Mrs Milligan's voice had grown feeble and thin. 'Lots of folk find themselves reliving those nights for the rest of their days. So much was lost, you see. But for some people there's more to it than memories.'

'Kind of supernatural, you mean?' asked Pete. All the hairs on his arms were standing up.

'I wouldn't know anything about that, son,' said Mrs Milligan. 'But I do know that Beth never came back here again. She never did get her box.'

'And every year I could hear her and her mother packing through the wall from me, just like you do, Pete,' said Mr Milligan.

'It's not really scary, is it?' said Pete.

'You're right, it's not. I'd say it's more deliberate, as though Beth and her mother want you to hear what they're doing,' agreed Mr Milligan.

'You say it stops, for the rest of the year?'

'That was my experience, Pete,' said Mr Milligan. 'Remember I told you about it the first time it happened to me when I was about five, Mother. I came running downstairs and said Beth's back but she's going away again. You dropped a big bowl on your toe.'

'And I couldn't hear anything. Thought you were making it up the first time. You never mentioned it again.'

'Until the next year.'

'And then it happened the year after that. That was when we realised she was coming back at the same time…'

'And only for a few days.'

The Milligans were speaking eagerly to each other, their voices rising.

'I know it sounds daft, but I got to look forward to hearing Beth's voice. I remember I used to think, "great, she'll be here soon".'

Mrs Milligan added, 'Because Jamie wasn't too afraid of these voices – and believe me, he was scared of plenty of other things – I didn't bother moving him out of his room. And I didn't want him to forget Beth, or what had happened to her.'

'You said the voices stopped?' said Pete. 'Why was that, d'you think?'

'No idea,' said Mr Milligan. 'I just remember that when I was sixteen or seventeen, there was nothing. And I missed it. You know, it had become something I looked forward to, like Christmas, or my birthday. I never heard the noises again…'

'Until…' interrupted Mrs Milligan,

'I'm getting to it, Mother. Look, I'll tell you quickly, Pete, but we're going to have to go. They'll lock you out of that home, Mother, if I don't get you back. You'll have to spend the night down here.'

'Tell him about Beth coming back.'

'As I said, Pete,' said Mr Milligan, 'the voices stopped when I was about seventeen. Every year I used to make sure I slept in that room for a few nights around the anniversary of the Blitz.'

'Even when you were away at university, Jamie. Very clever boy, you know, my Jamie.' Mrs Milligan's voice shook with pride.

'Anyway,' Mr Milligan butted in quickly, 'I would try to be around at the time when I had heard Beth before, but there was just a feeling of… nothingness, fresh air through the wall from me. For years it was like that: nothingness. Mother lived in the house on her own, – my father had died by then – and she heard nothing. We thought that was it. Beth was so far away anyway.'

'Did you tell Pete that she'd emigrated?'

'Don't think I did, did I? That was about five years after Beth left Clydebank. She and her father went to New Zealand. Auckland. Beth would be about fifteen or sixteen then.'

'And were you still hearing her through the wall?' asked Pete.

'That's the funny thing. The year she emigrated – I was about eight or nine – I heard her and her mother so clearly that it sounded as if they were in my room. That was the only time I found this whole thing a bit creepy. I was younger than you are now, Pete, and I remember looking out my window towards the air raid shelter one day and hearing someone open my door, walk into my room and speak. But of course, it was Mrs Winters coming into *Beth's* room through the wall.'

'I can still see your peely-wally face that morning, Jamie,' said Mrs Milligan. 'Beth's back, I said.'

'And she kept coming back, over the next few years, but the voices seemed fainter each time and finally, as I said, they didn't come any more.'

Mr Milligan sighed quietly, 'I wish I knew what she wanted.'

In the silence that followed, Pete let the story he had just heard sink in. He thought of Beth, her blue eyes and plaits, and wondered how he could help her. He jumped when Mrs Milligan clutched his arm and cried out in a bleating voice,

'Nurse. Nurse. I've no' had my pills. You've put the lights out and no one's given me my pills. And I need to go to the bathroom.'

Pete heard Mr Milligan move beside his mother, and speak as though to a child.

'Ssshh, Mother. Time to go. Let's get your pills.'

In his normal voice he said, 'Pete could you take my mother's other arm and we'll get her into the car. I shouldn't have had her out for so long. She was desperate to meet you when I told her you heard the voices through the wall. Almost like her old self again. I hope this doesn't set her back.'

'What's up, Mr Milligan? She was fine a minute ago.'

Mr Milligan spoke sadly, 'I wish she was fine. Probably forgotten who I am by now. Have you heard of Altzheimer's?'

'No,' said Pete. The group were shuffling up the garden now, Mrs Milligan leaning heavily on Pete and muttering about her pills.

'Most days Mother's like a baby again. Her memory's gone, and she can't look after herself. That's why she's in the home.'

'She was great when she was talking about Beth.'

'I know, she can have good spells, but that was the best one for ages,' said Mr Milligan. 'This has all just happened over the last year. She lived in your house – well it's her house really – until nine months ago. One day she switched on the gas and tried to fry bacon without lighting the pilot. Then she got herself into the bath and passed out. I found her, just in time.'

Pete and Mr Milligan were talking over the old lady's head as they made their slow progress though the garden.

'Explain to your mum and dad why I left, will you, Pete. We won't come in. I've to see your dad tomorrow about the site, and arrange for you to visit the school you'll be going to. Mrs McPhee, the rector, is my cousin.'

Pete groaned. 'I'd forgotten about school.'

'Best days of your life, sonny.' Mrs Milligan's head flew up suddenly making Pete jump. 'There's nothing to beat the three R's. You tell that Prime Minister, Tony Bear, that's what I say.'

Mr Milligan eased his mother carefully into his passenger seat and Pete stood by ready to close the door.

'Bye, Mrs Milligan,' he said.

The old lady looked vaguely at Pete as though she had never seen him before in her life. Mr Milligan started the engine and called across his mother, 'See you again, Pete.'

Suddenly the old lady fixed Pete with a penetrating stare. 'Mind you do what my Jamie didn'ae manage. Help that wee lassie so her poor mother can rest.'

CHAPTER FIFTEEN

PETE found his parents slumped in front of the television. Jenny was slung over his father's shoulder, while he banged her on the back to get her wind up. If Mr Smeaton stopped thumping, Jenny would cry until he started again.

'How d'you get on with Milligan, son?' asked Mr Smeaton absently, between thumps. His eyes were fixed on the news.

'Did he give you all the low-down on the school you'll be going to? Said he didn't need to talk to me because it was you he wanted. No idea why he had to bring his mammy along. Funny bloke, isn't he Jo?'

'Big smoothie,' said Mrs Smeaton in a lazy voice.

'His mum was OK. Really interesting, actually,' said Pete. 'D'you know, Dad, that this very night in 1941, when Mr Milligan was three, they were stuck down in the shelter while Clydebank was blitzed, and in the morning when they came out just about everything had been flattened?'

'Mmmm,' said Mr Smeaton, his eyes on the screen.

'And Beth Winters' house was destroyed. Y'know, that girl I can hear through the wall?'

'Really, Pete? Is this one asleep yet? We've not been able to put her down for the last two hours.'

Pete stared down at his father's head and looked across at his mother. Her eyes were closed.

'Jenny's awake,' Pete said loudly so that everyone in the room was forced to turn and look at him. 'She's staring right at me and I bet *she* heard every word I just said even if you didn't. I'm away to bed. Good-night!'

He closed the door with as near to a slam as he dared.

'G'night, Pete,' his parents chorused sleepily, ignoring his outburst.

'Be up to see you later,' yawned his mother.

'Yeah, right!'

Pete stomped upstairs to his bedroom, his footsteps echoing loudly in the uncarpeted hall. It was very dark, and beyond the cosy living room in which his parents sat, the house had an eerie feel to it. Pete was tempted to go back downstairs to join his parents, even if they were going to ignore him, but when he looked back at the way he had come, the hallway seemed even darker and less inviting. He flicked the light on in his room before he went in. Then he stood at the door and listened.

Silence.

A new silence.

Pete put his ear to different parts of the wall between his house and where Beth's had once stood, and sensed an openness – or what was it Mr Milligan had called it? – a *nothingness* – beyond the layer of bricks. He was sure that Beth's room had gone, slipping decades ago into the ruin and rubble of the shored-up gap-site next door.

Pete's bedroom was chilly. He climbed into his bed and as he threw his duvet over his legs, he saw Beth's notebook lying open at a page covered with drawings. This was one he was sure he had not read with Dunny either.

Beth had made a border of little faces all around the page. Each face was totally different, and full of character; men and women and children, drawn in very few strokes. They were good, very good.

'Cool artist,' said Pete, switching on his bedside light to have a closer look. Beth had used pencil and some of the sketches were fainter than the others. There were damp spots on the page and an earthy brown smell rose to Pete's nostrils.

Pete studied each of the drawings in turn. There was a woman with dark curled hair. '*Mummy*' was written underneath. Beside her was drawn a solemn man with a neat moustache and a walking stick. He seemed to be staring sternly out at Pete. '*My daddy*' was written in a balloon around the sketch this time. Then a smiling, curly haired child, wearing two bows at either side of his forehead: '*Jamie/Shirley M*'. Below him in the margin and looking up as though checking on the child was another woman, this time with loose hair and an anxious expression.

'That looks like old Mrs Milligan,' muttered Pete. He was right: '*Auntie Mary*' was written on a little flag above her head. Then there was a glamorous looking man whose image was encased in a love heart. '*Hugh*,' whispered Pete as he ran his nail under Beth's handwriting. The remaining border comprised about a dozen faces of boys and girls, each distinguishable; some freckled, some bespectacled, some dark, some fair, some smiling, others grim. Around three of these faces, Beth had drawn a thick double border, shaped like a tombstone. She had printed the letters *R. I. P.* beside their names: *Harry Small, Katy McNamee, Micky Kelly*.

There was a lot of writing in the middle of the page, which Pete recognised as the one he had started to read with Dunny in the shelter that morning. It was the last entry. He read:

13th March 4am.

It's horrible down here. Everything's crashing down outside. Really, really near. The ground's shaking, and everything in here is rattling. Even Mr Lyons' teeth.

I keep saying prayers to make Mummy and Daddy safe.

Auntie Mary's scared. I know because her face is all funny and twisted as if she's crying and smiling at the same time.

We're all just staring at each other, too frightened to talk. I keep seeing a picture in my head of Mummy putting those things into my box and I get a horrible, horrible feeling. Why can't she be here just now?

I'd nearly finished all my packing when the siren went off. Probably I'll have to fold everything again. Mummy brought me a Land Girl's outfit in Glasgow today. It's the best thing. The britches come just below my knees and button up. Daddy called them keek-catchers. There's a tie, and a jacket. Not as heavy as the real thing, but Mummy says it looks real enough and Aunt Katy'll put me out to work the farm when she sees I've got the kit. Hope so. Then I won't have to start that stupid new school. Mummy had better be with me my then, or I'll just come back by myself.

Please let this stop so we can find out who's all right.

I had to stop writing for ages then. There's been a gigantic explosion, and lots of wee ones. All right beside us. I can smell burning.

Jamie's screaming his head off in my ear, and Auntie Mary can't settle him. She's in a right state.

I'm going to draw him Aunt Katy's old blind dog bumping into something.

He liked that.

Well, I had to make him shut up because he was making me want to cry too. I told him about the things Mummy packed for me to take away. Would have been better if I'd showed him, but I think I left the box in the hall cupboard. There's cards from Hugh, and photographs of us all together. Mummy's wedding picture. A napkin from the kitchen. Mummy said it smells of home and she's right. She let me put in the ivory elephant that Daddy said was very old and came all the way from Africa. And the china bell from the hall. Mummy said if I ring it she'll hear it right down here in Clydebank. I know that's impossible.

This is the most I've ever, ever written in my diary.

This is the longest I've ever been down in the shelter. And the scariest.

Shells are landing so close. They won't let me go and see if Mummy's safe.

Hope none of my friends are hit tonight.

I hate this war.

I hate this shelter.

I want to get out of here, because Jamie has just dirtied himself like he always does, and the shelter is smelly stinky.

Maybe it was because it was late, and lots of strange things had happened that day, but Pete had to swallow to hold back tears which threatened to well up and land on the page on his lap.

'I wish I could have helped you,' said Pete, addressing the notebook. ''S not fair that you have to keep coming back here every year because Mr Milligan couldn't help you. I wish I could.'

Cold and tired, Pete wriggled further under his duvet without bothering to undress. He tried to kick off his shoes, but they got stuck half-on, half-off and he just left them like that. He lay back on his pillow, which smelt of London, and realised that so much had happened on his first day in Clydebank that he'd hardly thought of his old flat or his school or the friends he's left behind. It would be great to tell Simon and Alfie about Beth. Maybe he'd write to them.

Dreamily, Pete began to compose a letter in his head. It was difficult to think where to begin. He still held Beth's notebook limply open on his arm, his eyes going in and out of focus, as he stared at the faces she had drawn around the page. As his eyelids finally drooped and closed, the drawing of Beth's father with his stern face, moustache and walking stick seemed to bore into his mind.

Moments later Pete dreamt he was back in his old classroom, sitting beside, not Mira, but Dunny:

'What you doing here?'

'I've moved. My mum's got a new job.'

And Pete had a new teacher, or rather his old teacher, Mr Fielding, seemed to look like himself one minute, he even coughed – 'AHEM! AHEM! – in that ridiculous way when he wanted to get attention, but when he turned round from the board he was Aidan Winters, still saying 'AHEM!'

'AHEM! Now this is very important boys and girls. I have become a teacher because I was – AHEM – wounded in the First World War. How many of you have heard of it?'

Pete was trying to put his hand up, but it wouldn't lift. It seemed to be glued to his side, and he daren't shout out, although he was desperate to speak. He heard himself groan in frustration.

Somebody glided up to the front of the class, as though she were on castors. It was his mother, holding Jenny, dressed in a tiny school uniform. Mrs Smeaton was speaking in an actressy voice:

'The strange thing about that war – the Great War as we call it – is that just before soldiers died on the battlefield or in the trenches, many of them appeared to their relatives at home.'

Pete tried to interrupt but his mouth wouldn't open.

'You told me that. You told me that ages ago,' Pete was screaming inside himself so loudly that his head felt it was going to burst.

'I'm dreaming,' he heard himself think, 'but now I know why Beth comes back.'

Pete stood up on the desk in the middle of the classroom, and this time when he tried to speak his voice boomed out and he sounded just like Mr Milligan. He was wearing a suit and a greatcoat which swept the floor, exactly like Mr Milligan's had done in the cupboard, in fact.

'The dying wish of these soldiers was to be home with the people they loved best. Well, wouldn't you want that?' Pete turned and yelled into Jenny's face. She blinked back at him, and her eyes were Beth's.

Pete continued, speaking in Mr Milligan's voice. 'Most of these poor boys called for their mothers as they died, and I can understand that as I am very fond of my own mother who is ninety-three. That's why she always comes to school with me.'

With a sweep of his hand, Pete/Mr Milligan indicated old Mrs Milligan, who sat in a little corner of the classroom in front of a brazier, drinking milk from a bottle. She didn't look up.

'Although these poor soldiers lay dying far away from home, they appeared at the moment of death exactly where they would have wanted to be: sitting at their kitchen tables, walking in their gardens, or calling to their mothers or sweethearts. Now Beth Winters…'

As Pete was addressing the class, still as Mr Milligan, he noticed his father, dressed in shorts and a cap creeping into the classroom.

'Pay attention all of you, especially the latecomers, because you will be tested on this. Beth Winters is not dead, but she was removed, some might say against her will, to another place when she had unfinished business in this one. Her mother on the other hand was killed, and we know that she was trying to do something for her daughter. What was that thing, class?'

'Find her box,' everybody chorused.

'Correct. But she did not succeed. She too had unfinished business. Like the poor soldiers on the battlefield who do not want to leave this world far from their loved ones, Mrs Winters wanted to be near her loved one by giving her the box. I fear I may be confusing you, Pete.'

Pete was now sitting at a desk listening to Mr Milligan, who was spinning around in circles on the desk-lid wearing a judge's wig with pink bows in it.

'Don't worry about that big smoothie,' screamed his mother.

'My son Pete. He'll find that box. But he'll need to pull … pull off your sweatshirt. You're roasting. Come on, Pete. Lift your arms.'

Half-in and half-out of a woozy, dream-drunk daze, Pete felt his mother tug his sweatshirt over his head.

'You've been shouting in your sleep, talking in a big deep voice. And I bet you didn't clean your teeth,' said Mrs Smeaton.

Pete remembered to tuck his feet under his duvet so she didn't make him take his shoes off. He wanted to get back to his dream, but like all interesting dreams, it had gone.

CHAPTER SIXTEEN

PETE sat bolt upright on his bed.

Someone had called his name urgently.

At first, his mind processed the call as part of another dream, for there was a split-second delay before Pete was propelled from sleep to wakefulness. In the dark his alarm clock glowed the ungodly hour: 5.30 AM.

'Ohh,' Pete groaned, and let his head lead his heavy trunk back towards the soft, welcoming mattress. An inch from contact and the enveloping pleasure of sleep, he was summoned once more,

'Pete! Pete-Smeet!'

He shot up once more and looked around him, eyes staring wildly about in the darkness. He could hear his own heart knocking against his ribs; accompanied by a tattoo of fear drumming between his ears.

'Mum?' he called, his voice small and thin in the darkness. He wanted it to be his mum but he knew the voice was not his mother's, nor was it coming from inside his room.

His legs were wobbly as he rose, every follicle in his body standing to attention, awaiting the next call. Then it came:

'Pete-Smeet, please come down and help me.'

The voice was plangent. It rose, not through the wall, as Pete first thought, but from beneath his window. At first Pete saw nothing when he looked out. Darkness swam before his eyes, although on the horizon the faint washed-out blues of an early spring sunrise were beginning to relieve the night.

'Pete. Pete-Smeet. Down here.'

Pete scrunched up his eyes, searching for the source of the voice, and there it was. Beth Winters, wrapped in a tartan blanket, stared up at him with wide terror-stricken eyes.

Pete gulped. With shaking hands he opened his window and leaned out.

'What is it?' he hissed, 'What d'you want?'

Beth began to sob. 'Look what they've done. My house is gone. Bombed to bits.' She squealed suddenly as a rumbling noise grew louder and suddenly a huge explosion shook the ground. Pete felt the vibration through his arms.

'You all right down there, Beth?'.

'Uhuh,' came the tremulous reply. 'I shouldn't be out here, but it's so awful in that shelter. We've been bombed all night. Kept thinking the shells were going to land on us, but instead, they've landed on my house.'

Her voice rose to a tearful crescendo. 'And I don't know if my mummy and daddy are all right.'

Pete felt a surge of sympathy for Beth, and stared at the forlorn figure who stood before him like a spectre. More and more daylight was creeping into the sky and Pete could see Beth more clearly. A breeze had blown loose strands of hair from Beth's plaits and they whipped wildly across her cheeks. Pete remembered how one of the plaits had struck him as she swept boldly past him in the shelter. Now her face was deadly pale and streaked with dirt. There was no boldness left. And it was not just Beth's appearance that had changed in the dawn. Gone from Pete's perspective were the tiers of post-war houses which crenellated the horizon from his bedroom window.

Instead it looked to Pete as though Beth stood on the tongue of a monster with smoking ranks of irregular teeth. As far as his eyes could see were jagged buildings, ruined, burning. Swathes of smoke swirled around this scene as if a sinewy dancer weaved through the devastation trailing a large smoky flag. Here and there flames licked the sky, and elsewhere buildings slowly dripped stonework, raising huge sorrowful dustclouds.

Pete had seen pictures on the news, of towns torn open by war: Bosnia, Beiruit, Kosovo, but he had never experienced the horror of such devastation so close. He hesitated no longer.

'Hold on a sec,' he called to her. 'I'll come down and join you.'

The hallway was pitch black as Pete, slipping off his shoes to be as quiet as possible, groped his way downstairs and to the back door. He slid his hands along the walls looking for the light switch.

'Damn it!' he said aloud, 'I don't have a clue where the switches are in here.'

Beth was calling him again, 'Pete, are you still there? I need you to help me find my box.'

This was the first time that Beth had mentioned why she wanted Pete. Having given up on finding the light switch, he made for the kitchen window and rapped it. Beth was just outside.

'Be out in a minute,' he called, as loudly as he dared. Beth nodded in understanding and moved to his back door. He saw her silhouette behind the frosted glass.

'Just looking for the back door key,' he explained. He didn't want to waken his parents in case their arrival on the scene chased Beth away. 'It's not in the lock.'

Pete fumbled about the worksurfaces and shelves near the door, wincing as he sent some tins clattering to the floor.

'Damn!' he said. 'Beth,' he called through the keyhole, 'I can't get out. It'll be the same at the front. If I start poking about, my mum and dad'll come down.'

'Please help me, Pete,' called Beth. 'If you don't help me tonight, I'll have to wait another year for my box. I don't want to come back year after year. I'm getting too old. Jamie's never helped me, and next time I come there might not be anyone here at all.'

'I'm stuck in here, that's the problem,' said Pete, growing angry. 'The window won't open either.'

'Ooooh,' said Beth, impatience mingled with frustration. 'You'll have to try the tunnel.'

'Tunnel?' said Pete.

'In the hall, between our houses. Remember, stupid. You came through it this afternoon. In fact,' Beth clapped her hands enthusiastically, 'I've just remembered that the last time I saw my box was when we were talking down there. Remember?'

Pete was glad that he was looking through the frosted glass. He didn't have to meet Beth's eyes when he said, 'How can I get through to your house now? It's just been bombed.'

There was a telling silence from the other side of the door. Pete waited, angry, that he could not do more.

'Please try for me anyway, Pete.' said Beth at last, 'I don't want to keep coming back here.'

Beth's voice was persuasive enough, but it was the next thing she said which settled his resolve.

'I can't believe you actually came downstairs to talk to me. All those years Jamie Milligan would come to his window when I called him, but he never came this far. Just stood there looking down at me. Even when he was big. He was scared. I haven't been back for years, until last year, because he wouldn't help me. Last year, when I came, there was no one here. The house was empty. I've got to search one last time, because I don't want to keep coming back like this.'

'What d'you mean?' asked Pete totally puzzled. 'How do you come back like this?'

'Because… because… I want to. I need to. I don't know. OK?' said Beth, 'But are you going to help me, or not?'

Pete sighed. 'OK, then. So how do we do this?'.

'Right,' Beth's urgent voice rasped through the keyhole. 'You go through your part of the tunnel as far as you can and I'll see if I can meet you at my side.'

Pete exhaled nervously. 'You'd better be careful. Your house will be dangerous if it's just fallen. All that stone will still be settling. Don't climb over anything that looks wobbly or you'll end up crushed.'

'I'll be careful, Mr Sensible,' said Beth forlornly. 'But this is my last chance. I'm sure that box is near the entrance to your house. If you hadn't talked to me down there today, I might never have lost it. Think about that one.'

'Right, let's quit the chat,' said Pete, sounding a lot braver than he felt. He had no torch, and knew that he would be crawling in total darkness.

'See you soon, I hope.'

The cupboard door creaked menacingly as Pete opened it and peered inside. Blackness, utter blackness.

'Ungood,' he whispered to himself, as he began to edge his way though the cupboard. His bare feet caught splinters of wood, and his heel beds scraped on nails which protruded from the floor.

'This is horrible,' he shuddered groping his path with outstretched arms. As he sought the edges of the small door to the tunnel, a little voice at the back of his head was niggling, 'Cobwebs, cobwebs, there must be millions of them here. Sticking to your hair. Brushing over your face. You hate cobwebs, Pete don't you?'

'Shutupshutupshutup,' Pete chanted to himself, teeth gritted in tension. He just wanted to get this search over with. He shoved at the door on Beth's side of the tunnel. Earlier, it had swung easily into Beth's cellar. This time Pete had a problem.

The first thing he noticed was the smell: dusty, strong, as though someone had been flinting stones together. It billowed up into his nostrils causing him to splutter, while particles stung his eyes, making them itch and water. Then there was the door itself. It would only open a few inches; certainly not far enough for Pete to wriggle through.

It was dark on Beth's side, but not as dark as Pete's cupboard. Through the crack of the door he could make out large shadowy mounds, and in between these mounds there were thinner, more angular shapes. Looking up, Pete could see chinks of pink-tinged sky through gaps in the mounds.

'The whole house is down,' he said, forcing his face as far

in the door as it would reach. 'These must be the walls and ceilings and floors.'

The angular shapes were strips of wood, and fractured pipes from which tired streams of water welled. There was something horribly raw and new about the scene that made Pete want to recoil and run back upstairs to his bedroom, pull his duvet over his head, and pretend that none of this had ever happened.

But before he could quit he heard the scrape of someone moving gingerly over loose stones.

Beth stumbled towards him. She was talking and crying at the same time and the jolting of her body over the wreckage of her home distorted her voice, making it sound weird and wobbly and hollow.

'Pete, look what they've done. N-n-nothing will ever be the sa-ayme again. Can you see what they've do-one?'

Pete's limited view of Beth's shattered home was obliterated as a pair of dirty scraped legs slid into his view from somewhere above him. This was followed by a large chunk of stone which Beth must have dislodged as she made her way towards Pete. It missed Beth but struck the door out of which Pete was peering, slamming it shut against his temple. Dazed, Pete swayed back on his hunkers, rubbing the swelling on his head.

'Ouch,' he complained.

'Pete,' called Beth in a frightened voice, 'Please don't go. Wait, I'll just see if I can...'

'There!'

Triumphantly, Beth swung back the door of the tunnel and faced Pete. She had managed to make the opening much wider than Pete had done.

'You must come through now. See what they've done.'

Still dazed, Pete crawled into the ruin.

'Wow!' he said, looking upwards. He and Beth were standing in a tiny clearing at the bottom of a jagged circular enclosure of teetering, groaning stonework. Pete could sense the imminent possibility of everything collapsing on top of them both.

'You're crazy to have climbed over this lot,' said Pete. 'Just listen. This is all going to come down.'

Beth's voice was desperate.

'Well, come on then. Let's look quickly. The box must be under here somewhere.'

Her voice reverberated around the complaining ruin. As Pete shook his head despondently and started to say, 'There's no chance...' a wooden beam suddenly leaned forwards and propelled itself towards Beth.

'LOOK OUT,' screamed Pete lunging forward and shoving Beth out of the way of the missile as hard as he could.

'Dhuh!'

He heard the breath knocked from Beth's back as she hit a table with a dull thud. The force of Pete's shove hoisted her right over the table and on to a pile of wet rubble with her legs in the air.

'What d'you do that for? Bet you saw my knickers.' said Beth, outraged.

'I didn't want this to happen to you,' said Pete. He felt his face flush. He was angry at her ungratefulness, and embarrassed because, of course, he had had an eyeful of Beth's knickers.

'Look.'

The beam which had missed Beth had glanced off Pete's foot as it landed, gouging out a large chunk of flesh.

'Oh no,' said Beth, I'm sorry, Pete. I shouldn't have made you do this. That looks really bad.'

'One minute,' said Pete. 'Then we're both out of here. It's far too dangerous to hang about; we could get crushed under this lot and I don't suppose there's anyone about to rescue us.'

'Everyone's in the shelter. I just snuck out,' said Beth.

'Right then,' said Pete, 'This is where I saw you earlier when you had your box.'

'Over there, that's where I sat,' pointed Beth, 'but it's all covered with stones and stuff now. Oh look, there's a bit of my mummy's bedcover under that window frame.'

She began to cry again, so Pete moved forward. Blood was pouring from his injured foot, and it stung like mad. He daren't look at it.

'Over there, you say,' he spoke briskly, trying to sound brave and determined. 'If there are any gaps in the stones, I'll try and get my arm through and wriggle it about a bit. We might just be lucky.'

Pete didn't feel lucky, as he lay on his stomach and tentatively fed his arm as far as it could go into the opening closest to him. This was where Beth thought she had last seen her box. She squatted alongside Pete and sucked on the end of her plait. Pete dabbed his palm gingerly over floor of the cavity, praying that his fingers would not be crushed by a stonefall. He felt glass and sharp pieces of stone. The ground was wet. He kept patting further, further away from himself until his fingertips met uneven boundaries created by fallen brickwork.

'Nothing here,' he said to Beth. His voice sounded hollow He realised that he had slithered right into the cavity with his eyes shut, so that his whole trunk lay under a pile of teetering masonry.

'Yikes, this is mental,' Pete whispered through gritted teeth as he carefully slid back out to face Beth.

'You're nuts to go under that,' Beth said as Pete emerged panting with relief and wiping the sweat from his forehead. Admiringly she added, 'But you're dead brave. Those stones are all loose.'

'Really?' said Pete hoping sarcasm would hide his blushes, 'I hadn't noticed.' Then more kindly he said, 'Listen, Beth, there's nothing here. We should go.'

Dismay crumpled Beth's face.

In the background a wailing siren started up, its shrillness muffled by the columns of stones around Pete and Beth.

'That's the all-clear,' said Beth, wearily. 'Bombing's stopped.'

Pete wasn't listening to the all-clear, however. His ears were tuned to the slipping and cracking nearer at hand. All around him a little orchestra was playing in Beth's damaged home; slip, creak, crack.

'We've gotta move now. This lot's all going to come tumbling down on top of us.'

Beth looked around her wildly.

'I can't leave without the box. Please, its really important. My mummy…'

Beth looked pleadingly into Pete's eyes. As he stared back amidst the devastation, hearing the droning all-clear, he thought of the tragedy still to come for Beth. He averted his eyes from her pale, blue stare and concentrated on the strangely grotesque sight of half a bath. It was turned upside down, and it's smooth white underside stuck up in the air like a big round backside. It had claw feet at the bottom. Pete thought it looked a bit like someone who was trying to wriggle though the stones, but couldn't get their giant bottom through. There was a little grotto created by its upturned position which seemed free of debris. Pete crawled over to it and leaned into the hollow. 'It's the Bath Cave,' he said making his voice echo around him, shocked at how his mind decided to throw a joke at him at a time like this. He shuffled forward on his knees until his whole body fitted the curves of the bath. Once more he started to feel around with the palms of his hand.

Beth had crawled in behind him. Pete felt her breathing down his neck. He shivered.

'Anything? Anything there?' she asked, her voice cut by the hollow of the space.

'Shhh,' Pete snapped, 'I'm-just-seeing-how-far-I-can-reeeee-ach.'

Sweat prickled Pete's temples. He sensed the imminent danger in what he was doing. Two more seconds in here, he promised himself, extending his fingertips as far as they could stretch.

His entire body trembled with the effort of balancing in such an unnatural position. He had wriggled forward until his face was flattened against the front of the bath, his lips mashed against the overflow grille. Meanwhile he had slipped his hands under the rim of the bath and they were blindly seeking anything which resembled the edges of a box.

'Please don't let the bath land on my fingers, please don't let the bath land on my fingers,' Pete prayed as he groped around. He was just about to give up and say to Beth, 'There's nothing,' when his fingertips pushed something away. Something that might have been a box.

'Damn,' he said into the overflow, and strained to make his already overstretched fingers stretch that little bit further. His back was in spasm. He could not stretch any further to give his fingers more leverage. Only the luck that had evaded up until now finally let him pinch the corner of whatever he had found between his thumb and forefinger and drag it a little way towards him.

'Beth,' he whispered, not daring to turn around in case his hand moved away from his position. 'I've got something but I can't get a grip of it with one hand. Can you slide in beside me and get your hand underneath the edge of this bath?'

With difficulty Beth squeezed herself alongside Pete. As she tried to force herself further in, her head clunked hard against the enamel bath, making it rock. Pete and Beth held their breath as stones shifted above them.

'Careful, Beth. Don't move any more. I'm going to push something against your hand, you try and get a hold of it. Then we'll both get out of here as fast as we can.'

Beth lay on her stomach and stretched her arm under the rim of the broken bath exactly as Pete had instructed. She had to press her face into the ground to give her arm maximum reach.

'That's my hand in as far as it can go, Pete,' said Beth. 'I can feel something in here? D'you think it could be...?'

Pete didn't answer.

'I push, you grab. NOW!'

Beth squealed a delighted 'Yesss' in Pete's ear as something slid from his grasp to hers.'

At the same moment the ruin above them gave a huge rending shudder. Beth and Pete withdrew their heads from the bath and looked upwards as the Winters' home disintegrated around them.

'Beth! Move!' screamed Pete as huge hunks of stone rained downwards glancing off other stones on their way to the ground.

This was a moment of unforgettable fear for Pete as he cowered helpless and trapped, ducking bricks, glass and metal. The tones of the all-clear still droned in the background and the cacophony was compounded by the screams of a woman and child somewhere high above Pete's head.

'Beth, Beth! Are you in there Beth?'

Through a cloud of dust, Pete saw Beth beside him, clutching a box.

She raised her head up and yelled.

'I'm here, Auntie Mary. I'm fine. I'm coming up.'

Pete felt something being pushed into his hands, and heard Beth saying, 'I'll get this later today. Need two hands to climb up here.'

Then she darted forwards and kissed Pete noisily on the cheek, saying, 'You shouldn't say damn. It's very rude.'

As Pete stroked the spot on his cheek which burned where her lips had touched, Beth scrambled upwards like someone attacking a stony downwards escalator. Pete could only stare wide-mouthed as she traced a swift path way through the shifting stones and disappeared out of sight.

Then anything that had not fallen yet tumbled downwards with a great tired crash. Pete fell to his knees and scrambled in reverse to the opening of the tunnel which led into his own house. He kow-towed to the landslide above him protecting his head as best he could with one arm while the other cradled Beth's box against his chest. The doorway to the tunnel was narrower than ever: a pipe had wedged itself along the bottom of the door. Pete managed to shove Beth's box through the opening then inserted himself one leg at a time, insinuating himself along and around the door as though he was a large misshapen snake. He had to suck in his stomach to get it to go through. Now only his head and his outstretched arms remained on Beth's side.

Stones rained down clunking off his wrists and knuckles, and glancing off his temples as he pushed himself back through the doorway.

Pete began to panic. He tried send a ripple of movement through his whole body in an attempt to make himself slither through more quickly, but he was tired. He heard himself grunt and pant with the effort.

'C'mon, push, push!' he urged himself. Suddenly he felt the door yield a fraction and he slid back a bit further into the safety of the dark tunnel. Only the top of his head and his left arm from the elbow downwards remained outside.

'Go! Go!' he grunted, desperately forcing himself backwards. He was doing it. He was getting through: move move mo…

Pete never saw the brick that knocked him out. It struck his temple and bounced to the floor just as he withdrew into the dark cavity between the houses. As he collapsed, the weight of his unconscious body pushed the tunnel door closed for ever.

CHAPTER SEVENTEEN

A WOMAN was speaking. Miles and miles away. Pete couldn't hear what she said at first. But then her voice grew louder.

'Where's my girl? Where's my girl?' The voice was half-singing.

'Where's my girl?'

Clomp Clomp Clomp

A thought forced itself into Pete's mind. He knew it was the first thought to come into his mind for a long time. Because it hurt. Behind his eyes. There had been nothing but darkness for ages. Now there was this throbbing thought. And it was a worrying thought.

'That's her mum. She's looking for her. If I go out and stop her maybe she'll be all right.'

But it hurt too much to think, and Pete didn't know how to lift up his head. The effort of trying made a hammer beat against the inside of his skull. The pain suddenly drew up a big wave of sickness from the middle of Pete's stomach, and it heaved into his mouth and he vomited.

'Uggh.'

Pete heard himself groan as he recoiled and tried to move his face away from the foulness at his cheek. When he hauled himself up, his head bumped against something and that made the pain worse.

He heard the woman's voice again. This time it was closer, and it was singing.

'Who's my girl? Who's my girl? Who's the loveliest girl in the world?'

The voice was closer now, somewhere behind Pete. He knew the voice, knew it well.

'Mum.'

Pete's voice didn't sound like Pete's voice; it was faint and small. He tried to clear his throat.

'Mum. MUM.'

'Pete?'

Mrs Smeaton had heard him. The relief Pete felt at being discovered boosted him enough to crawl a little way towards the exit of his cupboard. He was so dazed that when his arm knocked against Beth's box, he pushed it clumsily to one side. His injured foot felt as though it had been pumped up like a balloon.

'Pete? What you doing in there?'

Mrs Smeaton was trying the light switch.

'Can't see in here. Uggh. It stinks. Pete, are you all right?'

Mrs Smeaton's voice grew increasingly anxious as Pete crawled towards her feet. He heard someone groaning and realised that it was himself.

'For heaven's sake, Pete what's wrong with you. I can't see you in there. Steve! Steve! Come and help me. There's something wrong with Pete.'

Pete winced as the stairs creaked above his head and his father bounded down, taking two or three steps at a time. Pete thought they were going to crash down on top of him.

'Steve, there's something wrong. Pete's lying in the cupboard and he's been sick. Oh, no he's covered in blood.'

Pete heard his father's voice, but it sounded all far-away and echoey. Jenny was crying, but she sounded miles off too. Pete lost consciousness again when he felt his father's warm hands grasp his shoulders, and squeeze reassuringly. That's when he knew everything would be all right.

When he came round the second time, it was very busy in his lounge. There were two men dressed in green boiler suits leaning over him, and behind them hovered his parents, and Mr Milligan. Pete was lying on the settee. There was an elderly man in a suit fiddling about with his foot.

'Pete? Pete can you hear me?' One of the men in green

was slapping his face, and calling very loudly into it at the same time.

'Pete! Pete! Open your eyes again, sonny.'

Pete tried to oblige, although he would much rather have gone on sleeping, and found himself looking at two huge noses which slowly resolved into one, still huge. Everyone in the room gasped with pleasure at the same time.

'He's come round,' Pete heard his mother say. She crouched down by his head, Jenny in her arms.

Mrs Smeaton had been crying; her eyes were all red, but she was smiling at the same time.

'Oh, Pete, what happened to you? How did you get so badly hurt?'

Every word his mother said took a few seconds to sink in. Pete felt as though his brain was travelling back from a faraway place.

He opened his mouth v-e-r-y slowly and tried to talk.

'Beth came last night. Said she needed her box. I got it for her.'

He was speaking through thick jelly. Everything was all floaty and strange.

'Shh,' said Mrs Smeaton, frowning worriedly at his answer, 'Maybe you should just rest.' She turned round to the others in the room and whispered loud enough for Pete to hear, 'He's talking rubbish.'

'Not surprised. Been through the wars, this wee lad,' said the green man with the big nose. He turned to his colleague who was about to take Pete's blood pressure.

'Serious laceration to the foot, contusion to the head resulting in period of unconsciousness. Signs of concussion here, Archie. Vomiting, confusion, not to mention heavy bruising to the arms and trunk. Need to give the cops a bell, Archie. Tell them to meet us at the Sick Kids.'

'No! No!'

Pete was struggling to sit up, but he just couldn't find the strength. He had heard and understood everything the paramedic said much more clearly that time. The fuzziness was melting away, as though Pete was gradually waking from a particularly deep sleep.

'Nobody hurt me or anything. Don't get the police. It was an accident. I can tell you what happened.'

'Son, you need to go into hospital. In a case like this where we don't know how you came by your injuries, we need a police statement from you and,' he turned to Mr and Mrs Smeaton and sniffed disapprovingly, 'the folks who were meant to be lookin' after you.'

Pete interrupted in his normal voice, 'Ahah! *I* know what you think,' he said, sounding much more normal, 'I've watched Casualty. You think my mum and dad did this to me and that I'm too frightened to tell the truth in case I get put into care. So you think I'll tell you a pack of lies and you'll go away all worried and then two weeks from now I'll be brought in to the A&E with a broken arm and a black eye and this time I'll get a social worker to look after me and they'll come an interview my mum and she'll confess and…'

'Malky', the paramedic taking Pete's blood pressure snorted, concealing a chortle. 'Don't think this one's suffered any lasting brain damage this time. Why don't we hear what he's got to say?'

'What about his head and this foot, Archie?' said Malky, grimacing.

The elderly man who Pete did not recognise spoke up.

'The foot needs stitched, but I can do that for the boy just now if you like. The head injury's more of a worry. Pupils look fine, but I'd like to have look at the bump to his temple, and I can do it all more quickly here than in hospital. Save the NHS some money too.'

Silenced, Malky looked accusingly round the room, hoping to get support from someone else. Mr Milligan came forward and put an arm reassuringly around Malky's shoulder.

'This gentleman here,' he said, indicating the stranger, 'is Mr Hugh Winters. He's a surgeon.'

Hugh Winters grinned without looking up from Pete's foot.

'Stitched up more weans in the last fifty years than you've answered 999 calls,' he said, and went on, 'Now. Pete, if you tell us how you came by these knocks, it'll take your mind off my embroidery down this end. Just going to give you a wee injection.'

'Ouch!' said Pete. The prick of the needle pricked his memory.

'Wait a minute,' he said, eyes widening. 'You did say Hugh WINTERS?'

'That's my name, don't wear it out.'

Pete looked at Mr Milligan, 'Is he? Is that?'

'The very same,' Mr Milligan nodded. 'Beth's brother. He's in Scotland to meet her. Phoned me late last night, after I took Mother home. They're going to the Memorial Service today with my mother and myself.'

'What Memorial Service?' asked Mrs Smeaton.

'They?' asked Pete.

'There's one held every year in Dalnottar Cemetery for the people who died in the Blitz.'

'Haven't been home for years,' explained Hugh Winters, as he stitched Pete's foot. 'Don't live in these parts any more. Once or twice I used to try and go with my father when he came over from New Zealand. We lost my mother in the Blitz on the second day, you see. This is her anniversary.'

He seemed to be concentrating particularly hard on Pete's foot as he spoke, avoiding eye contact with anyone.'

'I'm sorry,' said Mrs Smeaton, looking from Hugh Winters to Pete and to Mr Milligan in bafflement. Of course, Pete thought, she doesn't have a clue about what's going on.

Hugh Winters continued, 'My father's ashes are buried with my mother, here in Clydebank. I brought them back over from New Zealand twenty years ago, when he died, but my sister has never visited the grave. Her children were very small when my father died and she couldn't leave them and come over. So this is the first time we've attended the Memorial Service together.'

'I was just driving Hugh past to have a look at the house when we saw the ambulance outside,' said Mr Milligan, quietly. 'Told him all about you, Pete, and what's been happening.'

'What d'you mean, "what's been happening"?' snapped Mrs Smeaton at Mr Milligan. 'Have you got something to do with my son being hurt?'

'Jo!' said Mr Smeaton.

'Well, he was outside talking to Pete for ages last night. Certainly wasn't about schools. Think I'm stupid? And then this happens. Maybe *we* should call the police.'

'No need,' said Hugh Winters calmly, without looking up from Pete's foot. 'I reckon you could say that Pete was just another casualty of the Clydebank Blitz. One of the lucky ones, too.'

There was puzzled silence.

'Aye,' said Archie, eventually, scratching his head, 'yon Blitz hit everyone around here. Everyone knew someone who was killed. I lost my great-grandfather. My grandmother used to say the angel of death knocked on every door.'

'I'm fae Edinburgh; what are yous all on aboot?' said Malky. 'What's the Blitz got to dae wi'the wee fellow's knocks? You going to tell us, sonny. Better make it quick.'

Pete was feeling completely clear-headed now, although he did have a thumper of a headache. He took a deep breath and began.

'Before the Blitz, Dr Winters' family lived through the wall from this house. His mother wanted Beth, that's his sister,' Pete pointed at Dr Winters who inclined his head in acknowlegment – 'to evacuate. But while she was packing, the bombing began so she had to go down to the air-raid shelter. Her house got flattened during that raid and she had to go away the next day without any of her stuff.'

'What the heck has all this ancient history got to do with

your cut foot, sonny?' sneered Malky.

'Beth didn't want to leave in the first place; didn't want to leave her mum – your mum,' he said looking again at Dr Hugh. 'She was afraid for her.'

'No wonder,' said Mr Smeaton, softly.

'Her mum had packed a box full of things to remind Beth of home, and Beth really wanted to have it. Then her house was bombed, and she had to leave without it.'

'And my mother knew how much it meant to Beth,' said Dr Winters. 'What Beth didn't know until after my mother was killed, is that my mother had put in letters as well as daft wee things. I mean nothing was expensive in the first place, but everything was really valuable and important to Beth and my mother. Some of the letters were from me. I used to write to her while I was at sea. My pals used to kid me on that I'd a sweetheart back home, but it was really my wee sister I was writing to. Pretended it was a big blond I'd met at the dancing. My mother always thought it was important to say what you meant when you got the chance, and I know she'd written things she wanted Beth to know, and Beth never got those things.'

'My mother was heartbroken that Beth left without her box, and later that day, after Beth left, she came to see if she could find it.'

'And that's when she was killed, wasn't it?' added Pete, very quietly.

Hugh cleared his throat. 'Didn't ever make it to the house.'

The room was silent, no one quite knowing what to say.

It was Pete who spoke up.

'The thing is – and I did try to tell you, Dad – that I've seen and heard Beth Winters. But she's still a girl, my age. And she said she's been coming back here for years to try and get her box.'

Pete couldn't help glancing at Mr Milligan when he said this. Mr Milligan caught Pete's eye and lowered his head sheepishly.

'Oh, come on, son,' interrupted Malky.

'Let him finish.' said Archie sharply. 'You go on, wee man.'

'Mr Milligan told me she used to come back at this time of year when he was a boy.'

'That's right, Pete,' said Mr Milligan fielding the surprised looks in the room with a shrug. 'Should have done what Pete did years ago. I'm ashamed of myself, when I see how Pete acted the first time Beth asked him for help.'

'What?' Mrs and Mrs Smeaton chorused, turning to Pete in confusion.

'Last night Beth begged me to help her. She called me downstairs. And I went. And that's how I ended up like this,' explained Pete.

'What did you do?' asked Mr Smeaton, 'I didn't hear anything.'

'Remember I was telling you about getting through into the house next door, only you said there wasn't a house?'

'Yes,' said Mr Smeaton rather sheepishly.

'Well last night I went through to Beth's house again. Except it had just been bombed and it was all collapsing. Beth was with me, in a real state, and we tried to find her box. We'd both seen it earlier, you see. I thought – although I didn't tell her – that even if it was there, it would have been all smashed to bits, but,' Pete suddenly grinned broadly from ear to ear and looked triumphantly at every face in the room, 'we got it. I found it. All the bricks and stones were falling down on top of us, but we crawled under a bath and we got it.'

Pete's voice rang with delight as he relived the moment of discovery. Then his smile disappeared.

'Hang on though: where is it now?'

'The cupboard you said?' Mr Milligan bounded out of the room.

'You still haven't explained your injuries, son.' said Malky.

'I told you,' said Pete, exasperated. 'Everything was

collapsing on top of us. Big stones. Sharp things. Must have got hit with one of them. But I'm fine.'

'And a collapsed building you say? Better gie the Council a ring.' That was Malky.

'Och Malky, ye puddin', it was during the war, for goodness sakes,' said Archie in frustration. 'Don't you listen to what anyone says? Nothing collapsed last night. It happened in 1941. But he was there. These are war wounds. It's fantastic.'

'You're as bad as he is.' spluttered Malky in disgust. 'War wounds. How can I put that in the accident report?' The two paramedics squared up pugnaciously. A punch-up was only averted by ecstatic whoops from the hallway.

'Yessss!!! At last, Pete,' yelled Mr Milligan. 'You've got Beth's box.'

CHAPTER EIGHTEEN

IT WAS a plain brown shoe-box, bound with string, a bit battered, with a split on one corner of the lid. Hugh Winters, who had finished bandaging Pete's foot, took the box from Mr Milligan and gently rubbed his finger across the label on the side.

'They don't make shoeboxes like this any more. Imagine anything like that surviving today?'

He read the label, smudged over with years of dirt:

Gentleman's brogue. Col. Black. Size 10$^1/_2$.

In a quiet voice he said, 'I remember when my father got these shoes. He always moaned about having to buy a pair when he only had the one foot. He'd stuff old rags and newspaper into the bottom of one shoe so it would stay on his false leg. He bought these for my cousin's wedding.'

'At the reception he was dancing a foxtrot with my mother, and he must have taken a corner on the dancefloor too quickly, because the shoe on his dummy leg came flying off and hit my Aunt Katy on the head. I can still remember her face as the shoe came flying through the air. Clunk. She'd a lump the size of an egg at the back of her head and a cut lip because she bit the glass she was drinking out of when the shoe hit her. My father wouldn't dance again that night, he was so embarrassed. Fact,' Hugh added 'doubt if he danced again. That was way back at the beginning of the war, just before I left for sea.'

'Can we see what's in the box?' asked Pete, eagerly.

'Oh now, Pete,' said Mrs Smeaton, 'I think Dr Winters will want to go through all this stuff in private.'

Hugh nodded his head in agreement.

'Even I wouldn't look through this box. It isn't mine. It's Beth's,' said Hugh. 'Sorry folks.'

Malky shrugged. He and Archie gathered together their equipment.

'We'll leave you people to it,' said Archie. 'That's some adventure you've had son. C'mon Malky. Let's go.' Archie left the room with Mr and Mrs Smeaton.

'Keep an eye on the wee lad,' he told them, 'especially over the next twenty four hours. If there's any change in his condition, take him down to casualty. The doc in there'll tell you what to do about his foot.'

Pete listened to the paramedics speaking with his parents, their voices gradually receding as they moved outside. He was left in the room with Hugh Winters and Mr Milligan.

'Pete, you're some lad,' said Mr Milligan, 'only here one day and you did what I could have done if I hadn't been such a feartie.'

'Beth's going to be over the moon,' said Hugh. He was standing at Pete's feet holding the battered shoebox.

'This is all that's left of her childhood,' he said. 'She keeps promising her grandchildren that one day she'll show them the things that were really special to her.'

'Grandchildren?'

Pete was shocked at the idea, thinking of the girl with the plaits and blue eyes. 'She's the same age as I am.'

'Only when you see her,' said Mr Milligan. 'She's nearly seventy now, with a grown-up family.'

'That's right,' said Hugh. 'Husband was an architect, like your dad. Retired, of course. She's got two children – well, they're not children now. One daughter's a doctor, that's Jean. She's the one with the children. The other girl paints, just like Beth.'

'She was good at drawing, wasn't she?' said Pete to Mr Milligan.

'She got even better,' said Hugh. 'She's well-known in New Zealand. Very collectable apparently.'

Pete shut his eyes and tried to picture Beth as he had seen her last, scrabbling over the debris of her ruined home. In his mind's eye he tried to replace the girl with the image of a plump floury-haired grandmother, wearing an artist's smock, dabbing paint from a palette onto a canvas. The image did not seem to fit with the Beth he had met. He could not imagine her old at all.

'Pete!'

He was drifting off to sleep.

'You all right?'

Hugh Winters was lifting one of his eyelids and taking his pulse.

'Come on, Pete, try to stay awake for me. Otherwise I'll have to get you admitted to hospital.'

Pete tried to drag his mind back to a waking state. He heard Hugh Winters voice calling him from the end of a long tunnel. Then he heard a door slam somewhere outside.

'That's the ambulance leaving,' he told himself, pleased at how clever he was.

Someone came into the room and smacked his cheeks. It was a bit sore. Why couldn't they just let him have a nap?

'Oi, oi. Stop it,' Pete heard his own voice, although it sounded miles away.

'Pete. Pete.' That was Dr Winters. He was a good guy, but Pete wished he'd stop smacking his cheeks when he was only trying to get some kip. Didn't they realise he'd been up half the night? Mum was there too, asking if he was going to be all right. She sounded worried. They were murmuring together, the low rumble of their voices making him sleepier than ever.

Pete tried to force his eyes open. Everything was all swimmy and funny. He heard the door bell but it sounded miles away. Inside his head he was in one of those films where the screen starts to ripple and you go back in time while a harps plays arpeggios; bloo, bloo, bloo, bloo…

'PETE!'

What now? The voice shouting in his face was more excited than worried.

'Pete open your eyes, wake up. Look who's come.' Mr Milligan was slapping Pete's cheek this time, for goodness sake, nipping him, and shaking his arm. Mr Smeaton was there too.

'He doesn't want to come round.'

Dad sounds panicky, thought Pete.

Then another voice spoke.

'Oh, he'll wake up for me. He's got to wake up so I can thank him.'

Strange accent, thought Pete, as someone kissed him gently on the cheek. He jerked up to a seating position and opened his eyes like Frankenstein's monster on the operating table.

'Steady on, son,' said his father, putting a supporting arm behind Pete's back. 'Take it easy. He looks as though he's seen a ghost.'

'I'm no ghost,' said the new arrival squeezing beside Pete on the settee and taking his hands in hers. With difficulty Pete focussed on a pair of pale blue eyes.

'Remember me?'

It was the woman in the strange floaty clothes, all soft purples and green and blues. The woman who had stopped Pete in the street twice the day before and asked him if he had 'found it' in that strange accent. Behind the exotic inflection of English spoken with a soft New Zealand accent, Pete heard Scottish tones too.

'Beth,' he said. 'You're Beth. Why was I so dumb? You just look the same.'

The woman laughed, 'That's the sweetest compliment this old lady's ever been paid in her life. Sorry I didn't get the chance to explain what I wanted. I couldn't figure out how to ask if I could come in and rummage through your house.'

Pete said to his mother. 'This is the woman I told you about, the one who came round yesterday.'

'Mmm,' said Mrs Smeaton rather tartly. 'I wish you'd told Pete who you were and asked him to speak to an adult in the house. He knows not to talk to strangers.'

'I'm know, and I'm sorry,' said Beth, looking round the faces in the room. She shrugged, 'I suppose I thought my request was so strange, and I was so... I don't know so churned up about being back here after so many years and seeing the house like this. I always hoped that this box would turn up. Guess I was shocked when I realised how unlikely that was.'

With her arm she gestured towards the window and beyond:

'Clydebank has changed so much. All these new houses springing up, and shopping centres everywhere. So busy. So much traffic. Nothing seems the same any more.'

'Sixty years of change,' interrupted her brother, 'all cities and towns are different, except for where you live now.' Hugh put his hand up to his face and whispered mischievously to the assembled company, 'She's not used to modern living. Stays in a tiny wee town where everything's forty five years behind. I mean, just look at her clothes. She still thinks it's the sixties. That's what keeps her looking so young.'

Beth laughed. 'I suppose I am a bit behind the times. Hugh's right. Where I live now the pace has always been nice and slow. We just got our first video store a few years ago. But as for my clothes,' she looked down at her loose shirt, 'That's just me. Take it or leave it. I've always liked bright colours. The stuff I used to wear when I was young was so heavy and itchy and tight. I mean, remember those barbed wire jumpers Aunt Katy used to knit and send down every winter?'

'Knit us into more like.' said Hugh, 'And she made us balaclavas that Mother made us wear in the cold.'

'Cool, like in the SAS,' butted in Pete.

'Not nearly as trendy,' laughed Beth. 'Ours always had big bobbles on them.'

Pete studied Beth. Her voice was young, and her eyes were young. Even her hair was young. It was still in the Princess Leia style, only faded blond. She caught Pete staring at her and smiled.

'Thanks for helping me,' she said. She lifted the shoebox on to her lap, and laid her hands on the lid. Pete noticed that the hands which fingered the string knot which had held the contents of her most special things together through so many years were bent and wrinkled.

All eyes were on Beth.

'I'm scared to open this,' she said quietly. 'I've tried to remember what was inside for so long.'

Hugh glanced at his watch. Mr Milligan did the same.

'Listen,' he said, 'we'll need to be off. I've to pick up Mother for the Memorial Service.'

Hugh put his hand on Beth's shoulder and said gently, 'We should go, too.'

Beth was far away with her thoughts, her hands gripped tightly around the box.

'What did you say?'

'It's time.'

Beth stood slowly. 'I'll look at this later, I suppose. No wait, there's one thing in here…'

She sat down again and fumbled with the knot. Hugh opened his medical bag and handed Beth a pair of scissors,

'Beth, we haven't time just now.' He sounded embarrassed as he tried to hurry his sister up.

Beth snipped the knot. Discreetly, Mr Milligan and Mr and Mrs Smeaton left the room.

'We'll be in the kitchen,' said Mr Smeaton, closing the door behind him.

Beth wasn't listening. She had removed the lid of the box gently and was parting the shroud of tissue paper which had once protected her father's brogues when they were new and which her mother had wisely kept to wrap the contents of the shoebox.

Pete, trying not to be nosy, half-closed his eyes. Underneath the red napkin with the gold thread, he'd spotted cards and letters, photographs, bits of cloth, tiny wrapped packages all disturbed as Beth rummaged distractedly though the box. She seemed oblivious to the presence of Pete or her elder brother as she mumbled to herself, 'Where is it?'

In frustration she tipped the box upside down over the blanket covering Pete's legs, and began to sift more urgently through the pile spread out before her. A faint smell of scent, slightly stale, had risen as the box was overturned. Pete noticed a small bottle of perfume which rolled to the end of the settee. He slapped his hand down and stopped it before it fell to the floor.

Hugh took it carefully from him and put the bottle to his nose, inhaling deeply.

'That's my mother's smell,' he said in a faraway voice. He slumped down heavily beside his sister and put his arm around her shoulders, keeping his other hand to his nose as he passed the scent bottle back and forth in front of his nostrils, taking deep draughts.

'There it is,' said Beth. 'I knew it was in here.'

She held out a photograph to Hugh and leaned on his shoulder.

Pete keeked around Beth's body and saw the back and white wedding photograph in a small tarnished frame.

Here were the newly-married parents of this elderly brother and sister sitting beside Pete. The young woman in her fashionable flapper's dress, with her long beads, bobbed hair, ivory cigarette holder. At her side, the solemn, elegant man wearing his medals from the Great War.

'Dad always talked about this picture,' said Beth to Hugh. 'He told me once that when he shut his eyes he couldn't see my mother's face any more although he dreamed about her every night. Said they kept on living their lives normally while he was asleep, but he had forgotten her face. On their wedding day, he said she was so beautiful he couldn't speak to her. He just stared. "I wish I could get her to smile at me, just once," he'd say to me. When he was stuck in bed before he died he used to tap the table beside him and say, "If I had that picture, I'd put it there." And he kept staring at that spot as if the picture *was* there, by his bed. I started a painting for him because I remembered this picture myself and he talked about it so much that I thought I could do it from memory. But the funny thing is, I couldn't remember her face, either. I'd forgotten how pretty she was... she is.'

Beth held the photograph out to Pete. 'Isn't my mum pretty?'

Then she smiled and ruffled Pete's hair.

'Everyone thinks their mum's pretty, don't they?'

'But she was, is, pretty, I mean,' said Pete. 'She looks like an actress in one of those old silent films.'

'Louise Brooks,' said Hugh standing up. 'That's what my father used to say.'

'Pete won't have a clue who that is,' smiled Beth. 'It's my Carly she really looks like. Wait till I show her this. I've told her about it a million times.'

There was a knock on the door.

'Sorry folks, if you want a lift, we'll have to go now,' said Mr Milligan, 'or we'll miss the Memorial Service.'

The contents of the box were scattered all over the settee, spilling on to the floor. Beth and Hugh began to scoop things together.

'Look,' said Mr Smeaton, appearing in the room with Jenny. 'Let us do that for you. We'll make sure we get everything together, and we won't peek. You come back here after the Service. On you go.'

Mr Smeaton ushered Beth and Hugh towards the door.

'I'll be in the car,' called Mr Milligan impatiently. 'Mother'll think I'm lost. Take care, Pete. Steve, we'll need to talk work later. Can't let this war halt production.'

Suddenly the small living room was empty and Pete looked down at the scattered cards and knick-nacks before him. It all looked so drab and old and unappealing.

'So this is what she's been waiting for all these years,' muttered Pete, shaking his head. Casually he opened a faded card with a loveheart on it:

To the prettiest little sister in the West. Missing you. Happy Valentine, love Hugh xxx.

Pete remembered sniggering with Dunny over this. It didn't seem funny at all any more. Carefully he put the card back in the shoebox.

Mrs Smeaton helped Pete to collect the rest of the things that Beth had tipped out.

'I can't begin to understand what's gone on here since we arrived,' she said, laying the last thing into the box and putting it on the sideboard. 'But this house feels much brighter this morning. Different. I feel better too, and listen,' she cocked her ear towards the door,

'What?' asked Pete, frowning. 'I don't hear anything.'

'Exactly,' said Mrs Smeaton. 'Our Jenny hasn't cried for hours, and she's wide awake. Just looking round. Smiling. She even smiled at me, can you believe it?'

Mrs Smeaton put her arm around Pete, 'Now if we can just get you back on your feet, maybe this new start is going to work out all right for all of us.'

That day, Pete recovered slowly. His parents wouldn't let him get up at first in case he fainted, or died. Nor would they let him have anything to eat or drink for hours in case his condition worsened and he had to get a general anaesthetic. After all he'd been through Pete considered this a bit much.

'Wish those paramedics *had* taken me to hospital instead of leaving me here,' he grumbled to anyone who tiptoed into the room to check if he was still breathing during the day. His parents just answered, 'Get some rest.'

They wouldn't even let him watch the telly in case the movement on the screen made him dizzy.

There was one concession. Late in the afternoon, Dunny was ushered in to see Pete with the warning, 'Don't tire him out. He's been through a lot.'

'Watcha,' said Dunny trying to sound English. He had called in on his way home from school, unaware of the drama that had taken place that day. When he saw Pete sprawled on the settee bruised and bandaged, he switched to his usual vernacular,

'Jeezo, man. What happened to you?'

'Dehydration,' said Pete faintly, 'They won't give me food or drink.'

'Here,' said Dunny rummaging in a satchel strangely devoid of school books, but stuffed with wrestling and playstation comics.

'Have some ginger. I've only had one swig. Swear there's no grogs in it.'

Pete was so thirsty he ignored the bit about the grogs, and after one endless drink he gasped, 'That's doesn't taste of ginger. It's Irn Bru.'

'Aye. That's what I said. Ginger. All fizzies are ginger up here: Coke, Pepsi, Lilt, Irn Bru – all ginger. Thought you were half-Scottish. Don't you know nothin'? Never mind all that, though, tell us what happened to you.'

Pete wondered, when he began telling Dunny of his adventures, whether he would believe everything that had happened since they had seen each other last night. Dunny stood fidgeting and biting his nails while Pete talked. He only interrupted when Pete told him about the Winters and Milligans going to the Memorial Service at the cemetery and Beth taking the wedding photograph with her.

'We said prayers in school today for all the folk who died. I've got relatives up there. Those great uncles I told you about.' Then he went back to gnawing his nails.

'So,' said Pete, when he had finished, 'what d'you make of all this?'

'Wish she'd talked to me. I'd have helped her no problem,' Dunny said, gallantly. 'She must have pure wanted that box to keep coming back every year. Imagine your dad's boss ignoring her like that. What a sin. And it's dead weird to think she was growing old on the other side of the world but was young here. I don't get that.'

'Neither do I. And this… this is what it was all about. See over there, that's the stuff she wanted. It's just a load of old… old… sort of junky things. Bits and pieces.' The words had exploded from Pete before he realised he was going to say them. 'Old pictures, scraps of paper, letters, trinkets and stuff. Dead boring. Thought there would be MONEY or something the way she kept going on about it all the time. Probably shouldn't have risked my neck for stuff like that.'

Pete spoke bitterly, surprised to find, deep down, that he was disappointed the box had not yielded more interesting things.

'Where is the box? Bet the stuff's dead interesting,' said Dunny.

Pete flung his arm out casually in the direction of the sideboard.

''S that old brown thing over there. Mean, look at it. Would you have crawled though all that rubble for that?'

Dunny didn't answer. He tipped the lid of the box gently with one finger and peeped in.

'We've not to touch it,' said Pete, 'She's coming back for it later.'

Dunny wasn't listening. He had bent his knees a little and had stuck his nose just inside the box.

'Ahh,' he said, exhaling slowly. 'That smell.' He stuck his nose inside again and breathed exactly the same way as Hugh Winters had done with the bottle of perfume.

'That's my granny's smell. It's violets.'

'I thought grannies smelt of old crumbly mouldy things,' said Pete, although he knew this was unfair. His own, rather glamorous granny smelt of perfume and whisky and illicit cigarettes. But he was feeling cross with everything now. Today seemed to be one long anticlimax following his nocturnal adventure. And the Irn Bru had made him feel queasy because he had drunk it too fast on an empty stomach.

'My granny didn't smell crumbly,' said Dunny. He sounded offended, his voice straining as though he was trying to speak when someone had their hands round his throat, squeezing his vocal chords. Pete saw Dunny take a big gulp. He sniffed, wiped his nose on his sleeve and returned to the box to fill his nostrils with another draught of whatever he could smell there.

'If I shut my eyes,' he said, in a far-away voice, 'it's just like I'm back in her house, opening all her drawers, looking for treasure. Makin' a right mess. She used to let me do that. She never minded.'

Dunny turned and looked at Pete his face stern and earnest all at once.

'See all the stuff in here, Pete, how can you say it's not treasure? It's real treasure. Imagine your mum died. Just imagine that. And you lost everything. Not only her but everything that she used to have, things you remembered about her.'

'OK, so?' said Pete sullenly. He didn't like to think about things like that.

'Well, anything like this would remind you of loads of stuff. Even when you were old, like Beth is now. You'd never forget. Things someone liked, or wore. The way someone laughed Their smell.'

Dunny placed the lid carefully back on the box.

'I know. See, my granny died last year. And she was brilliant... she was just...' he searched for another superlative, '... just mega. And I've got a wee bag of stuff – a pair of beads she used to wear, a wee lavender fish she had on her mantelpiece, a card she gave me on my First Communion, stuff like that. My dad helped me to choose some things. OK, so you think it's crap but,' he shrugged. His voice sounded all wobbly, 'I don't.'

Pete put his head down and picked a ball of fluff from the blanket over his knees. He had never heard anyone his own age speak that way before. But he understood what Dunny had said about the things in the box, and he felt ashamed at his previous outburst. And he wished he'd told Dunny about the noises through the wall much sooner.

'OK.' he muttered into his drawn up knees. He was afraid to meet Dunny's eyes. Dunny came over and gave him a playful punch on the shoulder.

'Gotta go,' said Dunny, 'early dinner. Footie training tonight. Hey,' he was back to normal, 'maybe you could come next week, if your foot's better. Meet my pals.' Then he reconsidered, shaking his head gloomily as he studied Pete's foot. 'Big bandage that, Pete. Might be a couple of weeks. We'd have to stick you in goals – on the other side. See ya.'

Dunny loped out, cheerfully calling goodbye to Mrs Smeaton. A moment later he stuck his head back through the door.

'Hey Pete, see when Beth comes back, d'you think I could meet her?

CHAPTER NINETEEN

IT WAS evening before Beth and the others returned. Mrs Smeaton had decided by then that Pete was out of mortal danger and she let him get off the settee.

At first Pete's foot was so painful that he couldn't put his weight down on it without hopping up and down in agony on his good leg. This activity made his head throb where it had been hit. Otherwise he was on the mend.

He answered the door to the Winters and the Milligans when they arrived and wished he hadn't when, delighted at seeing him up and about, Beth and old Mrs Milligan – who seemed perfectly all right again – insisted on KISSING him several times. Pete, who did not let *anyone* do that any more, was still recovering from the kiss that young Beth had stolen before they parted.

Although everyone was dressed soberly – even Beth had cast a dark cloak over her colourful clothes – Pete felt there was a lightness about the visitors, a sense of relief, of completeness.

There was a similar lightness in Pete's parents' behaviour, too, especially now that they knew Pete was recovering. It had been like that most of the day. Mr Smeaton was full of energy, fixing up curtains and cooking a big bolognese in between calls to site staff and contractors. Mrs Smeaton seemed more cheerful and energetic than she had been for months. Pete would almost have said she was happy. In his subdued state, Pete was ultra-sensitive to the mood of well-being which seemed to resonate from every nook and cranny of his new home.

The visitors bore gifts: champagne and flowers for Mr and Mrs Smeaton, a doll for Jenny, who refused to look at it, and for Pete, from Beth, something he had wanted for a long time: a CD player.

'With this on,' laughed Mr Milligan (who brought Pete some rock and roll CDs), 'Beth'll have to use a power drill before you hear anything through that wall.'

'I don't need to come back again, though, do I?' smiled Beth. 'This is my thank you for what you did today, Pete-Smeet.'

Beth looked as though she was going to kiss Pete again.

'Can I go and show Dunny?' he asked his mother, quickly, bounding out of the room as fast as his bandaged foot would allow.

'Go on,' said Mrs Smeaton, laughing. 'Hop along. Tell him to come round if you like. Ask his mum when he's to be home.'

So the Smeatons had their first party in their new home. Eight of them squeezed around the kitchen table, all fighting to have turns of holding Jenny. Mr Smeaton had to ask Dunny if his mother could lend them a few extra chairs. Then it seemed only fair that she should join the party. Wee Stookie came too, and proudly showed off the cartoon on his plaster by the girl he had met in the garden yesterday afternoon.

The conversation could have returned to the events of the previous night, or the Memorial Service at the cemetery that afternoon, but it didn't. Instead everyone seemed to be talking about the future; what school Pete would go to after Easter. Would Wee Stookie always be so accident prone? (He tipped a plate of pasta on his lap at this point.) How Beth had a solo painting exhibition travelling to London from Auckland in two years, and how Dunny's mum would introduce Mrs Smeaton to her coffee ladies the next week. When Mrs Smeaton gave a saccharine smile and said she didn't drink coffee, Mr Milligan said he knew someone who was looking for a part-time administrator and why didn't he pass on her CV.

The kitchen was warm and cheerful. It smelt of bolognese

and coffee and resounded with many different voices and accents: Mrs Smeaton's London twang and Beth's Kiwi inflections which made most of her sentences sound like questions. Then there were the Scottish accents: Mr Milligan and his mother whose accents were distinctly Scottish, and then the tones of Pete's father and Hugh Winters who had had the edges of their Scottishness rubbed away by years in England.

Pete closed his eyes and let the chatter soak in. He felt very comfortable and dozy, his mind carried along by waves of conversation. He was on the edge of sleep when someone tapped his shoulder and a voice whispered in his ear.

'Pete-Smeet, wakey wakey. D'you think we could go down to your shelter and take a look inside before I go? I don't think I'll ever be back, you see.'

Pete's eyes worked more slowly than his brain in recognising the voice. They transported him to the previous night, and once more he was crouching inside the broken bath with Beth kneeling beside him. In his dreamy state of mind he found the tones of the young Beth in the voice of the old woman who was shaking him gently by the shoulder. Pete felt a great shiver run the length of his spine and when he opened his eyes Beth's softly wrinkled face was overlaid with his mind's image of the blue eyed girl with the plaits who had kissed his cheek.

'Whoa,' Pete roused himself, and sat up straight in his chair, 'I must have been dreaming,' he muttered. 'I thought you were still …'

'Young Beth? Oh, deep down somewhere I still am. Everybody's young inside.' Beth smiled at Pete. 'Would you mind, Pete? I'd love to take a look down there tonight, but I know it's your den now and I wouldn't like to pry. If you come with me you can make sure I don't touch anything.'

'Sure,' said Pete. 'Can Dunny come too? Most of the stuff down there's his. It was his before it was mine.'

He whistled across to Dunny who was in a world of his

own singing Tragedy to Jenny in a really, really creepy high voice.

'Coming out to the den? With Beth.'

'Ahh,' said Dunny in a disappointed voice, 'but I'm looking after the baby.'

'Suit yourself, Nursy,' said Pete in mock-disgust.

'Coming,' said Dunny thrusting Jenny into Mr Milligan's arms as though he was passing a rugby ball.

'These kids today are all the same,' said Mr Milligan, chucking Jenny under the chin. 'Just drop their weans and go and enjoy themselves without a by-your-leave.'

'Don't forget the torch,' said Mr Smeaton to Pete.

Away from the warm kitchen the night was clear and cold with a nip of frost in the air.

Beth had to go back inside for her wrap. As she swung it around her Pete remembered her business earlier in the day.

He asked, in a voice that seemed to cut through the darkness, 'How did you get on today at the cemetery?'

A burst of laughter carried from the kitchen.

Beth leaned on Pete's arm. She walked slowly.

'Thank you for asking, Pete. It was sad, kind of final. I was so glad I'd taken that photograph of mother and father with me, because it helped a lot. It's difficult when all that's left is an old gravestone . Yeah, but it was fine.' Her voice tailed off.

They had reached the door of the shelter.

'Oh, this place,' said Beth exhaling. 'The nights we ran down here. We would always know if the Milligans were in already because we would hear wee Jamie – listen to me "wee Jamie"; he's over sixty – crying as we got near. He hated this place. I used to be the only one who could cheer him up.'

'Like I do with Jenny,' said Pete.

'Me too,' said Dunny, affronted. 'She likes my singing. She goes all quiet and stares when I sing.'

'I've seen you both,' said Beth. 'I could have done with boys like you when my kids were driving me crazy. Oh look at this place. It seems so small now.'

Pete was flashing his torch around the interior of the shelter thinking of the experience he shared with Beth while the sirens screamed overhead and Beth and the other occupants huddled together in fear of their lives.

'I saw you in here, last night,' Pete said, his voice ricocheting eerily around the bare dark walls. 'You spoke to me. You wanted to get out. No wonder. It was terrible. And I heard your house falling.'

'I saw you too,' said Dunny, his words hanging in the darkness. 'Coming out of here during the day.'

'How come we could see you like you were during the war, Beth? And hear you. I mean I met you for goodness sakes, in your house. I crawled through that tunnel and talked to you. How did you do that? Why did you do that? D'you even remember meeting me?'

Pete had blurted out all the questions he could think of at once, but there was silence from Beth.

She did not even seem to be listening to the boys.

She walked around the shelter, paddling her fingertips along the wooden benches as though with each stroke she could absorb something from her past. She was whispering to herself, her shadow looming, a giant distorted shape on the wall as she caught the torch beam. Then she shrank into the darkness again.

'The Lyons and the Glancys liked this side. Probably hated all the racket we made, but they had to put up with it. Auntie Mary always sat here with Jamie. My mother and father and I liked this corner. I'd make my mother stroke my hair and tell me stories. It's a wonder she wasn't too scared to think. I don't think I could have coped down here with *my* kids.'

Beth slumped down on the part of the bench where Pete had seen her sit before, her back covering her own little cartoons and verses.

She drew her dark cloak around her. Pete swung the torch towards her, catching the paleness of her hair and face in its beam of light.

She still looks a bit like when she was young, Pete thought to himself, and still a bit sad, too. Beth did not know Pete was staring. She had closed her eyes, and rested her head against the wall behind her.

Pete felt uncomfortable pointing at her with his torchbeam and gawping. Dunny must have felt the same.

'Let's go,' he whispered, tugging Pete's sleeve.

Without opening her eyes, Beth spoke to the boys. Her voice sounded tired, and older than before.

'I can't remember seeing you boys, but the reason you saw me, I think,' she said, 'was that I could never leave here, not completely. Part of me stayed behind hoping to see my mother again, or at least find something that reminded me of her. I never let go. You boys will have no idea – and I hope you never will –, of how it feels to lose something that you love so much that you daren't imagine what life would be like without it. When I lost my mother, a bit of me could never grow up. After I emigrated with my father, I reckon my spirit stayed here in Scotland, even although I was physically on the other side of the world. That sounds crazy, I know, but I can remember times when I would be sitting on the beach in New Zealand, and I'd think myself back to Scotland. And I could be walking around in my old bedroom, or sitting in the shelter with my mother.'

'Mr Milligan – Jamie – used to see me a lot then, and hear me. But I could never get him to help me. Can't blame him, I suppose. Isn't it funny to think at that time, I would probably have been sitting in some classroom on the other side of the world – doodling or daydreaming when I was supposed to be working, and my mind would have thought myself back here. It drove everybody mad after a while. I had terrible problems in school because of it. Always in trouble, never paid attention to anything.' Beth gave a little laugh, 'Well, how could I if my mind wasn't with my body? My father had me seeing psychiatrists and educational experts, and doctors, but nothing helped me. Nowadays, I'd get counselling for – what'd they call it – stress… trauma… Missing my mum, and thinking about her, that's all that was wrong with me…'

Beth's voice tailed off in the bleak shelter.

Pete was silent. 'Think me back.' He remembered the words Beth had scribbled on the wall behind her head.

Slowly, he let the torchbeam, which he had pointed discreetly at the floor, drift to Beth's face. She smiled and looked at him.

'I must sound like a crazy old woman, telling you boys all this. I did settle down after a few years, and started to enjoy my new life, you know. But I could never forget what happened. I was always drawn back to Clydebank around the anniversary of the Blitz, and for a week or so, I would have no energy and I wouldn't eat. I would get sick and have to stay at home. My teachers and my father came to expect it. All I could think about at that time was my mother, and the last few days here before the Blitz. I would be back in my room, packing to go to Aunt Katy's, playing my recorder before that concert that never happened, and seeing my mother put those things in the box for me.'

'It's like you wanted to change what had happened so much that you sort of transported yourself here. That's pretty cool,' said Pete.

'Like Star Trek. Yeah, dead cool,' said Dunny.

'And it's like those stories of people about to die and they appear to their families back home,' said Pete, remembering his dream-theory. 'Maybe you just wanted something so much that you kept trying to make it happen. And it did.'

'Only it didn't bring my mother back, did it? That only happens in stories.'

'I think it's a scientific phenomenon,' pronounced Dunny, 'I'm going to try and find out about it down the library.'

'Yeah,' said Pete. 'Might have happened to other people.'

'I'm sure after something as horrific as the Blitz, there are lots of supernatural happenings,' said Beth. 'I can never bring my mother back, but you boys have helped me to find the bits of my life that make it complete, and you've no idea how much that means to me. And listen, don't think my life's been all sadness. Quite the opposite. There were times when I hardly thought of Scotland. I've got a sweet, sweet husband and two great kids, two grandchildren, *and* I became an artist, which is what I always wanted, after I decided not to be a doctor. All that doodling paid off.'

'Mr Milligan said you stopped coming back and he didn't hear you any more after a while.'

'They were probably the times when I was too busy chasing boys, or letting them think they were chasing me,' said Beth. 'I know that in the 60's and 70s I had my hands full with the kids, and I was painting. My husband was trying to get his business going and we were very busy. I still thought about my mother, of course, especially when each of my children was born, but time passes so quickly when you've a young family. Not that you boys will realise that for a long time.'

'Now it's my grandchildren who ask me all the time about my childhood. When I tell them about the box they say, "how d'you know it's not there, Granny? Go back and look for it again."'

'And you did!' said Pete.

'Yup, and this,' said Beth, 'is the thing I really wanted from that box – apart from the photograph of course.' She withdrew an envelope from her cloak.

'What is it?' asked Pete.

'Is it money?' asked Dunny.

Beth shook her head. 'It's just a letter to me, from my mother. She told my father it was the hardest thing she ever had to write. She wanted to put it in the box in case anything happened to her before she came up to join me in Beauly. Wanted me to know what she hoped for my future. My father said it nearly broke her heart thinking of me growing up without her.'

Beth clutched the letter in her fist.

'This is what I kept coming back for.'

The boys faced Beth awkwardly. The hand in which she held the envelope was shaking.

Pete glanced quickly at Dunny and then held out the torch to Beth.

'Here,' he said, 'We're heading back to the house.'

'Thanks, boys,' said Beth. 'I think I'll stay down here for a little while on my own.'

CHAPTER TWENTY

DUNNY told Pete that he could still see the torchlight through the crack in the bottom of the shelter door when he went home later that night with his mother and Wee Stookie.

'I thought of calling in to say bye, but I ...' he shrugged.

'I know, I didn't either,' said Pete. 'She stayed out there for ages. When she came in she was really quiet. She gave Hugh the letter to read. He went out to the garden for so long that Mr Milligan had to go and see if he was all right. Then they all left. They were pretty quiet. Beth gave my mum a big hug and the two of them started to laugh and cry at the same time.'

'Cringy. You go pure nuts when you're old, I think,' said Dunny sticking out his tongue, 'you must have been mortified.'

'What?' said Pete.

'Extremely embarrassed, Nigel,' said Dunny in a posh voice.

Pete shrugged, 'Whatever. Anyway they've gone. Beth's away back to New Zealand, with her box.'

'And all her happy memories of Bonnie Scotland,' said

Dunny in a romantic Shortbread-tin kind of voice, as he gazed into the distance. Then he thumped the ground with his fist, 'Ding, ding, your go. Hulk Hogan's going to get it now. And he's down!'

The boys were in the shelter. Beth had not returned, although a card had arrived for Pete that morning which read,

'Pete-Smeet, I'll never forget what you did for me. We'll keep in touch, love Beth.'

Beth had made the card herself. She had drawn a boy and a girl with long, blond plaits, crouched inside a broken bathtub. The boy was trying to push a box towards the girl. The background of the picture, sketched in charcoal, was a ruined house.

Thought she said she didn't remember meeting me, mused Pete to himself.

'She's a really good drawer,' said Dunny when Pete showed him the card,

'Think you mean artist, Dunny. Yeah, she isn't half. M'dad looked her up in some book at the library this morning and it turns out she's pretty famous.'

'You should hang on to that card then,' said Dunny, 'might be worth a lot of money one day.'

'I'll never sell it,' said Pete. 'Mum's going to get it framed for me.'

'Hey,' said Dunny, looking round the shelter, 'what about all these drawings Beth did when she was a girl. These could be famous, too.'

'You're right,' said Pete excitedly, 'like all those cave paintings that tell you about civilization zillions of years ago.'

'We could let people walk round here. Charge them to get in. Air Raid Art, we could call it.'

'We could make postcards.'

'Sell ginger.'

'We've still got that notebook. We could put that on display.'

'Could make a fortune, '

'We could take people tours of the ruin out there and give them one of those tapes that tells the story of what happened.'

'Then we'd have to take all our stuff out of this shelter.'

'Or it might get nicked.'

'We'd have to keep things tidy in here all the time. It'd be worse than my house.'

'And then who would look after it when we were at school?'

'We could just do it during the holidays like, to get some dosh.'

'But then we wouldn't be able to play.'

'And,' added Pete, thoughtfully, 'I don't think Beth would want us to do that to her shelter and her house. It wouldn't feel right somehow.'

'Bit of a hassle, anyway,' said Dunny.

'Let's not bother.'

'Nah, let's not.'

'And we should have given Beth back her notebook.'

'No way! 'S mine.' said Dunny, but while he was claiming ownership, he must have been thinking, too. 'S'pose you're right. We should give her it back. You should have given her it last night.'

'Forgot. I'd to ask you first anyway, didn't I? You found it.'

'I say send it back to her,' said Dunny with magnanimous finality, 'We'll wrap it up and take it to the Post Office now. Give her a surprise when she gets back to New Zealand. Why don't you see if your mum'll let us go down to the toyshop in the Centre. It sells wrestlers. I'll be allowed to go with you coz my mum thinks you're "sensible and very well spoken".'

'C'mon then,' said Pete, thinking that was the first time he'd ever been called sensible. 'She probably won't let me coz of my foot, but it's worth a try.'

LOOSE ENDS

THE INJURY to Pete's foot left a dramatic zig-zag scar although it healed up well and gave him a whole week without showers.

A year later friends still commented on it in the changing room after football training, or as Pete lined up to dive with his swimming squad,

'That's some scar, man, how d'you get it?'

'Glass. Happened years and years ago,' Pete would answer without elaborating.

He had gone to school with Dunny after Easter and settled in immediately. He had been afraid that people would make fun of his accent, but it must have been more Scottish than he thought. After a few weeks his mum was asking him to repeat things because she couldn't make out what he was saying to her.

'That's m'boy,' Mr Smeaton would say. 'I couldn't have put up with a Sassenach for a son. And Jenny'll always have a Scottish accent, too, won't you pet?'

Jenny would beam back at her father, as she beamed at everyone.

Mrs Smeaton said that she would always remember the anniversary of the Clydebank Blitz because it was also the anniversary of the night she knew she would get on with her daughter after all. Jenny was the happiest baby anyone could meet. Her nickname was Smiler and she charmed the pants off everyone, especially Dunny, and Mr Milligan. They became quite ratty with each other if they happened to be in Jenny's presence at the same time and had to share her.

Mrs Smeaton was happy, too. She had found a job, thanks to Mr Milligan's endless connections, and she never had to go to a single coffee morning. She got back into her tennis again, and managed to get to the semi-finals in her new club championship the first year she joined.

'Finals next year, Jo,' Mr Smeaton teased her, 'or we'll have to move back to England in disgrace.'

'No way, Dad,' said Pete. 'Who would run Milligan Construction without you?'

Mr Milligan had decided to retire. Although he was still technically the boss of Milligan Construction, he handed the day to day operation of the company to his new right hand man – Steve Smeaton. Since old Mrs Milligan was so frail, her son devoted hours to visiting her in the hospice. And it wasn't just devotion that kept Mr Milligan at his mother's bedside. He had a project on the go. He was trying to preserve his mother's memories of the Blitz, and the Second World War as a living record before it was too late. This was part of the work of the local history group he had joined when he retired. Old Mrs Milligan might be frail, but some days her mind was sharp as a tack. When she was 'on form' as Mr Milligan would say, she could remember just about anything that happened on a particular day, 'right down to the colour of her knickers...'

On her good days, her son would stroll up to see her with his tape recorder and microphone. At weekends Pete usually joined him, and the pair of them would listen spellbound as Mrs Milligan, and one or two other occupants of the hospice, brought the past to life. (It was no surprise that Pete won the history prize in school that year given that the topic was Life in Wartime Clydebank.) 'And you a White Settler too,' said Mrs Milligan when Pete showed her his certificate.

And Beth?

She did keep in touch with Pete and his family. She wrote to them regularly and telephoned from London when she came over to open her painting exhibition, sending them a signed copy of the glossy catalogue showing the paintings on display.

'Would you look at the price of these!' gasped Mr Smeaton flicking through the catalogue in amazement. 'Every one costs thousands.'

It wasn't the prices that shook Pete. It was the subject matter of Beth's paintings. She painted people photographically against a backdrop of war. Sometimes she depicted battle scenes, but more usually the aftermath of a bomb or a raid. Ruined houses, ruined gardens, ruined streets and buildings. The people in Beth's paintings were often children who stared out unwaveringly from the canvas with solemn impassive faces. The same faces appeared in all the different paintings on display. Those faces were those of Beth herself and of Pete.

The painting that arrived for Pete in time for his first anniversary in Scotland was not typical of the ones he had seen in the glossy catalogue, however. It was small, and simple.

It was of a couple on their wedding day; a slim, dark-haired bride with bobbed hair wearing a flapper dress, and a handsome moustachieoed groom in his uniform and medals. The man's face was carefully drawn, showing skin tones and the proud, hazel gleam in his eye. In contrast the woman's face was pale and indistinct, her features uncertain although there was a softness and a gentleness in the artist's brushstroke.

The back of the painting was inscribed:

To Pete-Smeet.
Thanks to you I can look on my mother's face again.

The back was signed:

from Beth, your neighbour.

Pete hung the picture on the wall between his room and Beth's. Beyond, Pete knew there lay nothing now but space. The jagged ruins of Beth's former home had finally been cleared by Mr Smeaton and Mr Milligan. Together they had filled the bomb crater with new soil and laid the seeds to a garden which would burst into flower in time for summer.

Pete knew that Beth had no need to return each March, but for as long as he occupied that bedroom, there were nights when Pete held his breath and let the hesitant notes of the Skye Boat Song float through the wall, played by his imagination.